PARALYSED

SHERRY ASHWORTH

PARALYSED

London · New York · Sydney · Toronto

A CBS COMPANY

SIMON AND SCHUSTER
First published in Great Britain in 2005 by Simon and Schuster UK Ltd
Africa House, 64–78 Kingsway, London WC2B 6AH
A CBS COMPANY

Simon & Schuster UK Ltd
Africa House, 64–78 Kingsway, London WC2B 6AH.

ISBN 1416900942

3 5 7 9 10 8 6 4 2

Printed and bound in Great Britain
by Cox & Wyman Ltd, Reading, Berks

www.simonsays.co.uk

For Sally

ACKNOWLEDGEMENTS

Thank you – to all those people who kept me on the right track, who answered my constant questions and told me their stories. And a big thank you to Fate, too, who threw Olwen in my path.

So – cheers! – Olwen Sisupalan, Sarah Stanwix, John Robinson, Nick Cave, Andy Lee, Neil and David Matthews, Derrick Jones, Stephanie Drake, Tom Somerville, Sara Menguc, Venetia Gosling, Stephen Cole – and Robyn and Rachel.

SIMON

I'm running. My feet are pounding the pavement, the wind's in my face, my arms are pumping by my sides, I'm breathing steadily. I grin at the kids coming towards me, run past them, and I'm over the crest of Ash Valley Road. Now I'm cruising downhill, letting the pavement carry me, faster and faster as the road drops ever more steeply. Beyond me are the hills, golden-green, reflecting the dying sunlight.

It's beautiful. I'm happy. My pace quickens, then steadies, and I'm almost flying along. I'm thinking about Danny's face tonight, when he walks into his surprise party. He hasn't got a clue, not a clue. None of us said a word. I smile as I imagine his jaw dropping and the girls squealing.

I reach the corner and swing round and the road starts to climb. There's the muted roar of the traffic on the main road. It's getting darker now; some cars have their headlights dipped. I had to come out for this run tonight. I couldn't just sit there doing nothing. I like to keep moving. It's getting harder now; I feel myself slowing, my legs heavy. So I push myself, feel my chest tightening, loving the sensation of the challenge, the sidelong glances of the passers-by who see me running – running up the hill, past the garage, the park on one side, the chippy on the other.

Then Emma flashes into my mind. I'm gripped by a special sort of excitement. It almost robs me of the power to run. She'll be there tonight. She'll tell me what she's decided. Hey, it's great to have a girlfriend and I still can't quite believe someone as lovely as Emma wants me. We're coming up to our six-month anniversary and, if she says yes, we're going to celebrate in a very special way.

I smile – I can't help it. The road levels and I cross the bridge over the railway line. As I run over it, a train approaches – destination Manchester – clacking over the tracks, getting louder, building up to a crescendo; but already I'm on the other side, in the home straight.

There'll be time when I get in for a wash, then the others are coming to my place half an hour or so before Danny. Emma's sorted it. I run more slowly now – cooling down – along our avenue and my mind strays to the weekend. Friday night tonight – and now the street lights are blushing into life – and it's Danny's party. Tomorrow morning I'm being rested, the school will play the match without me, because on Sunday – I wipe the sweat from my forehead as my body tries to adjust its temperature – on Sunday I'm playing for the county. An important match because the national coach will be there. Mr Smith says I'm in with a good chance. That's what I want – me in the national squad.

And now as I'm approaching home I'm buzzing with

excitement, thinking: bring it on! Bring it all on! I'm coming to the end of my run and the weekend's about to begin. I'm jogging now, jogging up the path, and see that no one's drawn the curtains yet, and there's David gazing moronically at the TV with his mouth open – typical of my younger bro – and I see Mum coming in to tell him something. They both spot me from the window and my mum's face brightens immediately.

As I stand waiting at the door I pull off my hoodie and jog on the spot. Mum opens up and asks if I've had a good run. She follows me in, tells me she's arranged to take Dad and David to Danny's parents for the evening so we could have the house to ourselves. Mum's enjoying the secrecy, I reckon. I'm pleased about that.

So it's up to the bathroom to shower, wash my hair, dress, peer in the mirror – and for just one moment I don't recognise myself. I'm getting older. True, it's Danny who's turning seventeen, and I'm six months behind him, but I see myself and know I'm not a kid any more. I run some gel through my blond hair and think of Emma. It's funny, when you know someone fancies you, you can see that you might be fanciable. I make a face at myself, a kind of tough, macho face. It makes me laugh. I squirt on some aftershave and go and get dressed.

I'm ready just in time. Mum, Dad and David depart, and they almost meet Emma, Jen and Steph coming up the drive. They're carrying bags and won't tell me what's inside them. 'A surprise for Danny,' is all they'll say. I seize Emma round the waist and kiss her. I ask her if she's reached a decision. She says, 'Wait and see.' She's gorgeous – long dark hair like in a commercial, laughing eyes, long lashes. The girls vanish into the kitchen and I go to put some music on. I try dancing a few steps. Not good. I can run, play rugby, footie, cricket; I can beat my dad at golf; I've abseiled, windsurfed and skied. But dance? I've two left feet.

A ring on the doorbell and it's Wilko and Adam. Why aren't I surprised to learn that Wilko's got the booze? I take their coats, and they ask if they're on time. The girls come in and we discuss how to play this. Should they all hide in the darkened front room and jump out from behind the sofa, shouting happy birthday? Adam says that's tacky. I agree. Emma says they should hide somewhere, and all come in and surprise Danny at a signal from me. Everyone said that would be better. So they all fly upstairs, jostling, laughing, then it goes quiet.

I'm thinking, this is fun, and I want Danny to get here as soon as possible. I glance at the clock. Nearly eight. Any minute now . . .

DANNY

A birthday is a number one excuse to get leathered – that's my philosophy. That was most definitely my intention on the night of the seventh of November, my seventeenth birthday. The plan was I would meet Simon at his place and we'd sneak into his local, where they weren't too bothered about under-age drinking. Not that you'd think Simon and I were under-age. Both of us are big lads. Simon's the blond, good-looking one; I'm dark, and not too bad, I suppose. My mother loves me, at any rate. At least for now.

So I was walking down Simon's road, hoping the cash in my pocket would last out the evening, humming a tune, when totally without warning I remembered what had happened at school that afternoon. Why does your memory do that to you? Break into your happy mood like a newsflash interrupting a favourite programme? *If things don't improve, I'll have to bring your parents in, Danny.*

My face scrunched up into a frown and I dismissed Mr Neale's voice. I returned to the tune, repeating the beginning again, walking more quickly, until I was slightly out of breath. To tell you the truth, I couldn't see the attraction in walking. If we were meant to walk, then we wouldn't have invented the car. I was looking forward to starting driving lessons now I was seventeen, but all that depended on the generosity of my parents. Would they be feeling generous after hearing what Neale had to say? Very, very doubtful.

Simon's house, at last. As I saw his front door in the distance I reckoned I might speak to him about what had happened at school. I slowed down as I thought that through. I don't like talking about my problems – it's a bit soft, isn't it? – but talking to Simon was different. He was my best mate and he understood me. Ever since we were kids I'd always felt he was on my side. That was why I was never jealous of him, despite the fact he was the school hero – a brainbox, tipped for both rugby captain and Head Boy, and boyfriend of Emma Shepherd. I reckoned if he had time for me, then not all hope was lost.

I rang Simon's doorbell loud and long. He opened the door, looked pleased to see me, and ushered me inside.

'You ready, then?' I asked.

'Nah, not quite. Couple of things I have to do,' Si said. 'But come in, make yourself at home. I've got a free house.'

I left my jacket on the banister and went into his front room. There was some music playing and the TV was off. Simon shouted that he'd get me a beer; I replied, 'Nice one!' Meanwhile I paced up and down the room, glancing at the Denham family portrait over the mantelpiece – Simon, David, his parents. There were trophies in the bookcase –

his dad's golfing cups, but most were things Simon had won. Just now, that hurt me. I realised I couldn't honestly say that my parents had any reason to be proud of me. But, hey, it was my birthday. I pushed all those uncomfortable thoughts from my mind. Simon returned with two bottles and we sat on the settee.

'Cheers,' he said.

'Cheers yourself.'

'So what did you get for your birthday?' he asked me.

'Money and stuff,' I said dismissively.

Simon bent down and dragged something out from under the settee and handed it to me.

'Wicked!' I said, and began to unwrap it.

I love getting presents. I could tell immediately it was something to wear. I had to tear the paper in the end and there it was: a rugby shirt.

'You trying to tell me something?' I ribbed him. Simon was rugby-mad; I didn't mind watching the occasional game. I like sport – as a spectator. I held the shirt up. It was an England shirt: white with a rose, the sponsor's logo, a red flash down each side. I checked the size. Extra-large.

'Cheers,' I said. I opened the card that was with it and it was suitably obscene. I chuckled at the joke.

'How does it feel to be old?' Simon asked me.

'You'll find out soon enough,' I replied.

We carried on drinking. That was when I thought about speaking to Simon about Mr Neale. We were alone and I was still sober. Only I knew that as soon as I began to explain the problem, I'd have to do something about it and that would mean a commitment. But avoiding the issue wasn't going to solve anything. I opened my mouth. Si, I was about to say, but then I noticed he looked distracted. He was listening to something outside the room. That stopped me.

'Hold on a mo,' he said, and sprang to his feet.

I was left alone. It was weird, being on the verge of spilling everything and then Simon just disappearing. Then I thought I heard voices. They got louder, Simon reappeared and, before I had a chance to work out what was going on, there they all were – Wilko, Adam, Jen, Steph and Emma – shouting happy birthday, laughing, whooping. I should have guessed.

Oh, what the hell. It was my birthday. Most definitely *not* a day to deal with bad stuff. 'Nice one,' I said to them, and then I was surrounded by the girls, asking me if I'd suspected anything, swirls of their perfume spicing the air, making me want to party.

EMMA

Danny's face was a picture. For a split-second he was lost for words. Then he started to grin. We were all so excited – more than him, perhaps. It's always like that on birthdays – you enjoy other people's more than your own. But we were all up for a good time that night. And the girls and I had cooked up a little surprise.

'Quiet, everyone,' I shouted above the noise. Simon went over to turn down the music. 'As you know, it's Danny's birthday. And me and Jen and Steph have all brought him a present. But he can't have it until he's completed our Birthday Challenge.'

'You what?' Danny asked, scratching his head.

'Our Birthday Challenge,' Jen chipped in. 'You've got to do three things – put on the clothes we've brought, eat one of our sandwiches, and spin the bottle!'

'But it's all right if you don't want to,' said Steph, spoiling it. She's one of those people who can't bear anyone to be upset or put on the spot. But she needn't have worried. I saw that gleam in Danny's eye.

'You're on,' he said. We all clapped and cheered. I could tell we were going to have a brilliant time. Everything was perfect. We were all together, all enjoying ourselves as much as you could, ever. And I was the happiest of all. I glanced at Simon and our eyes locked. My heart raced. My mum said sixteen was too young to be in love, but what did she know? The way Simon made me feel had to be love because I couldn't think of any other word that came close to describing it. That's why I'd made my decision. I knew Simon wanted it, but that's not why I'd decided. It was because *I* wanted to. And I was going to tell him that night when we got some time alone together. I shivered and felt nervous, almost like the stage fright I get before I perform.

But already Jen had dashed into the kitchen and returned with one of our carrier bags.

'You've got to put your hand in here and wear whatever it is you pick!' she exclaimed.

Danny finished his beer, put the bottle down, and felt around in the bag. I knew what was in there. An old bra of my mum's, Jen's silk underslip, and a pair of laddered tights. I could see Danny grimacing. His hand emerged with the tights.

'No sweat,' he said, tying them round his head like a headband. The boys cheered. Then he grabbed the bag from Jen and spilled the contents. He struggled into the bra and wore it back to front and threw the slip to Simon. Si put it over his head and it cascaded around his shoulders. But Simon is the kind of boy who couldn't look feminine if he tried.

Wilko brought Danny another beer and he took a long swig. 'Next, please?'

'You really don't have to do this,' Steph insisted.

'Yes, he does,' Jen said, an evil glint in her eye. Jen is Danny's ex and, although it's well and truly over, they always end up together at parties, then vow never again.

Jen came back from the kitchen with a plate of sandwiches. 'Pick one and eat it!' she commanded.

Danny grimaced, then winked at us. I couldn't see at first which one he took. They all had white fillings that looked like cream cheese. But one was face cream, one was Polyfilla and the other was toothpaste.

He chewed, then spat it out. 'What is it? Cement?'

'He chose the Polyfilla!' Jen squealed. 'Now, everyone, round the coffee table. We're going to spin the bottle. Whoever it ends up pointing to, Danny has to kiss.'

'No way,' Adam said.

'Boys too!' Jen insisted.

'If it's Si, Adam or Wilko, I'm doing without my present!' Danny said.

We congregated around the table. I set the bottle spinning. Round, round, round, more slowly now, slow-ly, it eased past Wilko, stuttered by Simon, and came to rest . . . directly in front of me.

I checked with Simon. I could tell from his smile that he didn't mind. It was only a game. As for me, I thought of Danny as a kind of brother. He was Simon's best mate and because of that I'd got to know him well. He's kind, generous, and just a teeny bit mixed up. I knew he was in some sort of trouble at school.

Then in one second it was over. He'd just pecked me on the cheek.

'No!' shouted Jen. 'You've got to kiss her properly.'

'It's okay,' I whispered. I saw him eye Simon. And then his face came toward me, the tights still tied round his head. Very softly, he pressed his lips on mine. It felt odd, but comfortable.

Immediately everyone was laughing and shouting, and Steph rushed into the kitchen to give Danny the CD and aftershave we'd clubbed together to buy him.

Danny had drunk a lot very quickly and he was wild. He was dancing with Jen while Steph was chatting to Wilko, who also had a bottle in his hand. Adam was with them. That was good, as it gave me a chance to be alone with Simon. Neither of us like to do the couple thing too much in front of our mates. We have nothing to prove. We managed, as the party got into full swing, to have a moment alone together, and I said to him, 'There's something I want to tell you.' He knew what it was about and took my hand. And just then Danny bounced over and grabbed Si.

I don't remember much else of the party; it was just a blur of faces and movement and loud music. But this one thing did happen: I was still waiting to have a chance to speak to

Simon. I noticed, at one point, he was no longer in the room. I was with Adam, who was showing me his digital camera. I excused myself and went to see if I could find Si.

The kitchen was empty and so was the small sitting room where his family watched TV. Simon has a lovely house – it's not posh or anything but it's always immaculate; his mum's more than a little house-proud. I sneaked upstairs and once I was on the landing I heard voices coming from Simon's room. Simon and Danny were talking to each other.

'So he threatened to kick me out of school.'

'No,' Simon said. 'He wouldn't do that.'

'Well, not in those words. But unless I get my act together, he'll call my parents in.'

'What's stopping you, Danny? Getting your act together?'

Simon's question was kind, neutral. I felt bad, eavesdropping. Then I thought: maybe I could help too. I didn't want Danny to be kicked out of school. We shared a lot of lessons, as we did the same subjects.

'Hey,' I said softly, pushing open the bedroom door more widely. 'I couldn't help overhearing.'

As I spoke, I felt a subtle change in the atmosphere. Danny grinned sheepishly. 'Just Mr Neale's way of wishing me happy birthday,' he joked. 'But no sweat. I'll sort it.'

'Tell you what,' Simon said. 'I'll see you tomorrow morning. I'm not playing, as they're resting me for the county match on Sunday. We'll hit town and go and spend your birthday money.'

I saw the quick flick of their eyes and knew that Simon would sort Danny out.

'Okay,' Danny said. 'I'll call around ten.'

'Sorted,' Si said.

'Let the party recommence,' Danny whooped, ran out onto the landing, and made as if he was going to slide down the banisters.

If you didn't know him, you'd think he was slightly mad. Which he was, at times. But I knew his manic exit was his way of letting Si and me have time alone together.

We hugged. I nestled into him so as he couldn't see my face.

'You know what we've been talking about?' I murmured. 'Well, the answer's yes.'

Simon's response was to squeeze me so tight I could hardly breathe. But as I said those words, I felt scared. Simon and I had talked about sleeping together, and he never pressed me, he said we should wait until I was ready. And I was ready. But I was still scared, in a good sort of way. I knew his family were going away in a fortnight and I would stay over. It would happen then. Simon entwined his hand in my hair and gently pulled my face to his and kissed me, long and softly. I knew I'd made the right decision.

I guessed it would change our relationship, but I didn't mind. I knew it would change me. I decided I wouldn't tell anyone, not even the girls at school, who were dying to know whether we'd had sex yet. Well, I might tell Steph – and possibly Jen. I would have to see how I felt.

'Hey, Emma,' Simon whispered. 'I l—'

'Whoah!' came a cry from Adam, who was halfway up the stairs on the way to the bathroom. Then he made as if he was going to snap us with his camera. We disentangled ourselves. Time to go back to the party.

For the rest of the night, what I did or said, I did or said with the consciousness that Simon and I were going to sleep together. I felt like there was an invisible cord attaching us, so that I knew exactly where he was and what he was doing without having to turn my head. I felt special. A different feeling enveloped me, a feeling that made me slightly weak and sleepy. I didn't drink much – I don't like the taste of alcohol. Simon doesn't drink much either. Even though rugby players have a bit of a reputation, he doesn't like what it does to him. But Danny and Wilko were well away. Danny had reached the stage where he had Jen on his lap and they were laughing together. Adam was telling Steph all about how he and his family planned to do their Christmas shopping in New York, which might or might not be true. Jen reckoned he was a bit of a poseur, but I just thought he tried too hard to impress. Like we all do. Simon with his rugby, me with my acting, and Danny always having to be the life and soul of the party. I was seeing everything so clearly that night.

I don't know what time it was when Simon's parents got

back. They took one look at Danny and Wilko, and Simon's dad said he'd drive them home. Steph's dad had arranged to collect the rest of us.

Danny was struggling with his jacket – he couldn't find where to put his arms. We were laughing at him.

'See you at ten,' Simon reminded him.

'Ten?'

'Yeah. We're going to town, remember?'

I smiled to myself. There was no way Danny was going to be up and out for ten in the morning. I've rung Dan at midday on the weekends and he'd still be in bed.

Danny seemed to come round for a moment. 'Ten tomorrow morning? Way too early,' he mumbled. 'I'll call in the afternoon.'

'The football,' Simon reminded him. 'What about Sunday afternoon?'

'Sunday afternoon,' Danny repeated, his speech a little slurred. 'See you then,' he continued. 'Good luck in the county match.'

'Come on, young man,' Simon's dad said. 'And if you feel sick in the car, warn me and I'll stop.'

They left us. I was holding Simon's hand. We said our goodbyes in public. I was stupidly happy, on cloud nine.

SIMON

I wake up and for a moment or two appreciate the warmth of the duvet and the birdsong outside. Then quite quickly my mind slips into gear and I orientate myself. I have a free Saturday morning because I'm being rested. Part of me doesn't like that. I'm out of rhythm, not being on the field on Saturday morning. I glance at my clock and see I've woken at the right time for this morning's match.

I remember Danny's party last night, but mostly think about Emma and what she said. But how can I wait two whole weeks? Two whole weeks! I need to stop imagining what I'm imagining, so instead I worry about Danny. I know he's not settled in the Sixth Form, but even before then he's fought school, won't try, avoids the challenge. Why? Is he scared of failure? I try to work out a way I can help him – yeah, I feel pretty sure we can sort something out. Whatever happens, there's always a solution. I feel my body filling with energy and know I can't stay lying here much longer. I hear someone finishing in the bathroom and I spring out of bed, realising I'm hungry and wanting breakfast.

I'm piling my spoon high with cornflakes when the phone

rings and Mum gets it. I can tell it's not one of her friends as her voice is too formal. She holds the phone in the air and mouths at me, 'Mr Smith. For you.'

Mr Smith is the team coach. Mum tosses me over the phone and I hastily swallow my cornflakes. Smith explains that Robbie Cairns has dropped out – stomach bug – any possible chance I could play today? 'Yes,' I say, without even stopping to think. 'Yes, of course . . . Yes, I'm sure.'

'Good lad,' he says.

I feel a surge of energy. I see the game as a kind of warm-up to Sunday, and like the feeling of being able to help out. Poor old Rob, though. This was meant to be his first chance to play centre in the A-team.

I explain to Mum what the situation is and ask if there's any chance of a lift to school. I can see I'm going to be late if she doesn't drive me. She's okay with that and shouts up to Dad – they decide to go shopping after they drop me off. So I wolf down my breakfast, get my kit, and before too long I'm in the back of the car, knees jammed against the front seat. Mum turns the radio on and we're moving.

The weather's good. There's sunshine, small clouds scudding across the blue sky, and the houses look bright and cheery as we accelerate down the street. I think about the match and even though it's only a friendly I find myself planning for victory – I'm psyching myself up. We drive past the park gates then stop at the lights. I feel impatient. I check my watch and can see I'm not going to have time to warm up properly. Not ideal, but it can't be helped. We're moving again and speeding off down the avenue. Then I have an idea – it would be good to see Emma, and so I get out my phone and text her to say . . .

EMMA

Hi babe. I'm playing this morning. Can you come and watch?

I smiled when I read Simon's text. No mention of what we decided last night – that's so typical of a boy. Like he hadn't given it another thought! And no love or kisses, just a matter-of-fact, come and watch me play. Lucky I know Simon as well as I do. He's not a sweet-talker, even though I secretly wish he was sometimes. But the fact he wanted me there at the pitch cheering him on spoke volumes.

I was going to settle down to make some notes for an English essay, but I had all weekend. I looked out of my bedroom window and it was the sunshine that decided me. I wanted to be outside. Never mind if it turned out to be cold. I'd wrap up warm, go down to school, and then maybe after the match me and Si could go somewhere and have some time alone. I wondered why Simon was playing after all and guessed someone would have dropped out. I worked out that if I got ready and left now I'd be there just after the beginning of the game.

I live quite close to school so it didn't matter that Mum

was at work. I made sure I locked up properly, took my phone and set off. I can't say I'm a rugby fan exactly and, despite Simon explaining the rules over and over again, I still can't quite work out what's going on until someone scores a try. There are just all these lads throwing themselves at each other and forming scrums and running with the ball, and Simon is generally in the middle of them.

I quickened my pace and thought about his text again. The fact he wanted me to be there was romantic enough, if you think about it. He could have easily just rung me after the game, but he didn't. He thought of me first. I smiled at the elderly couple walking towards me and they must have thought I was mad.

I reached school just after ten. The buildings were deserted and looked just like a stage set. School wasn't its bustling, crowded, chaotic Monday-to-Friday self, but tired red bricks, glad of a rest. I hurried down past the main buildings and on to the field. I could see the match had started. There were a few people on the sidelines: some other lads, teachers, a few parents, not too many spectators. That's because rugby is more of a players' game, or so Simon tells me.

I was nice and warm now from the walk and I took my place close to the pitch, but I wasn't naïve enough to think Simon would be looking out for me. When he plays, the game is everything. I completely understand that. It's like when I'm on the stage. I never watch the audience, I'm not even fully aware that they're there. What matters is that I *am* the character I'm playing. I have to lose myself completely. I reckon when Simon is on the pitch he loses himself in the same way. He's a machine that's designed to stop the opposition and get that ball over the touchline. You don't have time to think: how am I doing? Focus is everything.

I was thinking in this abstract way because I didn't have much else to do. I didn't know anyone watching the game well enough to talk to and I wasn't even sure when to shout or cheer. I kept my eyes pretty much on Simon, mud-spattered now and tousled. My eyes strayed over to the school roof and a V-shape of birds in the sky, travelling somewhere distant. Then I had one of those moments when I became completely aware of myself standing there – my hands in my pockets, clenched against the cold, chewing gum moving around my mouth, my hair ruffled by the wind – and I felt how real and solid life was. *I* was real and solid, locked into myself, apart from everyone around me.

I tried to turn my attention to the game again, only it was hard to work out what was going on. A scrum was forming. Vaguely I watched a mass of boys, pushing and shoving like some strange, multi-limbed creature not sure where to go, inching back then forwards. There were shouts from the sideline. I noticed Simon wasn't part of the scrum, but he was watching it, taut with energy.

The next thing, the ball escapes from the scrum, a dirty white oval. Someone kicks it up and under and it arcs into the sky. I watch as Simon leaps up with all the power in his body straight for the ball. But, no – someone else too – another boy has jumped and they collide in mid-air: I can hear the smash of bodies and I shudder. Then the referee blew the whistle, sharp, hard and long, and the game stopped.

I didn't know what to do. Of course I wanted to run over and speak to Simon but really there was no time. The ref was there, and the coach, and a few parents – proper adults, who knew what to do. I felt sick, my chewing gum like clay in my mouth. Then I saw the other boy get up and I was glad – I waited for Simon to follow.

There was no sign of him. Instead everything went very, very quiet. The breeze dropped. A cloud blotted out the sun. Something was wrong – there were hushed whispers from the parents and my stomach contracted with fear. I turned to the man near me and asked him what had happened.

'Don't know, love,' he said. 'Seems like the centre's hurt himself.'

Now I pushed my way onto the field. No one tried to stop me until I reached the knot of people around Simon. I caught a glimpse of him lying on the ground like a broken doll, his head at a strange angle. His eyes were barely open. Mr Smith was asking him questions, 'Can you feel this? Can you feel what I'm doing?'

Someone's mum arrived with a cushion and said, 'Put his head under this, he'll be more comfortable.'

'No!' Mr Smith shouted, and that was when I knew. You mustn't move a person if they've broken their neck. And that's what they thought might have happened to Simon.

'Oh, no, please, no,' I mouthed, and felt sobs rising, hysterical sobs, the sort that rip through you. Then a woman, a big, motherly woman, came over to me, and asked me if I was all right. I blurted out I was Simon's girlfriend and was he all right? She told me she was sure he'd be fine, and I'd had a shock, and she'd give me some tea from her thermos; and I found myself being led away from the pitch, and I was sat down by her on a canvas fold-up chair close to the pitch. I couldn't breathe properly.

I tried to see what was going on. I saw Mr Smith stand up and take his mobile out of his pocket. Meanwhile the ref shooed the rest of the players off the field. The game was well and truly over. Part of me wanted to be there with Simon, but the terrible truth is that I was scared. I was scared of what had happened to him. I didn't want to see it or know about it. I wanted the adults to sort it out; I wanted that woman to come back and tell me Simon had got up and it was all a false alarm and I was a funny one for having such a fit.

She did come back, but only to hand me a plastic mug of hot, sweet tea. I couldn't drink it. I kept straining to see what was happening. The woman stood by me. Her face was set and serious.

'He'll be all right, won't he?' I repeated.

'Oh, yes,' she said. 'Everyone knows what they're doing. This won't be the first time there's been an injury on the pitch. My Brian dislocated his hip last year and he's as right as rain now.'

I loved her for those words. Then I heard the *wah-wah* of the ambulance siren. Closer and closer. My stomach knotted again. I watched, shaking, as the ambulance drove straight onto the pitch. People backed away as the paramedics took over, bending over Simon, doing things that I couldn't see. In a few minutes they stood up and Simon was strapped to a red board-thing, and being carried swiftly past me, right past me, and I saw his face – he didn't see me. His eyes were staring vacantly and I thought: that's not Simon, that's his shell – and in a moment he was gone from me and the ambulance began its progress to the hospital.

I saw Mr Smith then and I jumped up. 'What's wrong?' I asked. 'What's happened to Simon?'

He stopped. His face was grim; there was no consolation there. I saw him take a deep breath. Mr Smith was a Maths teacher – I'd had him for GCSE. He knew about me and Simon – most of the teachers did. I could see he was trying to choose his words carefully.

'Simon's taken a bad fall and I suspect it's a neck injury. He says he has no sensation, but it's too early to tell for sure what the damage is. So don't worry. Please don't. Emma, do you have his parents' number?'

I was shaking as I repeated it. He walked away then and left me. Everyone was dispersing. A cold wind had picked up now and my hair whipped savagely round my face. No sensation? What did Mr Smith mean? Why couldn't Simon feel anything? That wasn't normal. Nothing was normal any more. I was trembling uncontrollably and close to tears. I wanted my mother, but she was somewhere on the shop floor. I thought of Danny. My shaking hands took my phone from my pocket and I selected his name. His phone rang, and rang, and rang. I got his voicemail. I disconnected and tried again. And again. And then . . .

DANNY

'Yeah?' I was so groggy, I didn't even check to see who was calling. It had taken me ages to find my phone among all the junk by the side of my bed.

'Danny? Simon's had an accident.'

Now I was fully awake.

'What do you mean, an accident?'

It was hard to make out what she was saying. The reception was bad and Emma's words were ripped apart by sobs. At first I thought she meant a road accident and I was scared. When she said it was in a match, that made no sense to me. He wasn't playing. He was being rested. Stupidly, I told her that. Then she explained – he was substituting and he'd called her to watch him on the field. Then he'd taken a fall and was carried away in an ambulance.

'Hold on,' I said to her. 'Don't be upset. That's always happening in rugby. 'S one reason I don't play. My life and limbs are far too precious.' I thought joking might calm her down and, to tell you the truth, I wasn't really worried. We were all too ordinary for bad things to happen to us. Bad stuff happens to people in soaps or other places, not to three normal teenagers living in the suburbs of a bog-standard northern city.

'No, Danny, he looked – weird, he wasn't moving. Mr Smith said he's hurt his neck. He said he had no sensation. Danny, I'm scared.'

'Where are you?'

'Still at school.'

'Shall I come and get you? Or do you want to come here?'

She said she'd come over and the line went dead. I swung out of bed and sat there with my bare feet on the carpet. My mind was racing. I thought over what Emma had said and although it was hard to tell quite how serious it was, what I picked up loud and clear was Emma's terror. It had cracked along the airwaves like a bullet, pierced me, and my blood was turning cold.

I flung on a sweatshirt and hurtled down the stairs.

'Mum!' I bellowed.

She came out of the kitchen, wiping her hands, and looked at me quizzically.

'Simon's had an accident.'

She frowned and I told her what Emma had told me. I didn't like the way her face darkened. I became aware that Katy, my kid sister, was leaning over the banisters.

'He's broken his neck?' she piped up. 'You mean like Christopher Reeve?'

I didn't know what I meant, but an image of Christopher Reeve flashed into my mind, strapped to a wheelchair, his smile out of kilter, a wax model of what he once had been.

'No!' It was a cry of despair. It came from me.

My mother took control. 'We need to find out what's happened. I'll see if I can get in touch with Sylvia.' She sounded deliberately calm. Sylvia is Simon's mother. Our mums have been friends for ages too – it was how we met, at a mother and toddlers' group, would you believe? My mum's an office manager. Most of the time I think she's a bit disappointed in me and I can't blame her. I've been known to give her a hard time. But just now it was like I was a kid again – and I wanted to be a kid again. I wanted to put the clock back.

'I told Emma to come round,' I added.

'Good,' she said. Already she was dialling on the landline. Time moved slowly. I watched her face brighten as someone picked up, and I listened to a half-conversation, not really able to make out what was going on. But she was off the phone very quickly and explained.

'That was David. Sylvia and John are on their way to the hospital now. He doesn't know what's wrong. I think I'll go and fetch him here too.'

Next she tried Sylvia's mobile. It was switched off. A news blackout. A total news blackout.

'If Emma's coming round, go and get dressed,' Mum instructed.

I followed orders. I washed and made myself presentable: all the time my mind lurching between hope and fear, despair and optimism. There was a cruel mockery in doing ordinary things: washing my teeth, automatically looking in the mirror and checking my hair. I wondered whether we should all go to the hospital. I just wanted to find out how bad it was.

Emma arrived and we sat together in the kitchen. She cried for a bit, then filled me in on everything. I didn't say what Katy had said about Christopher Reeve. I just listened and told her I was sure there was nothing to worry about. We could hear the TV from the next room, where Katy was watching it. Mum was already on her way to pick up David.

I don't know how many hours went past. All I remember of that day was the waiting. The clock hardly moved. We waited for the phone to ring, we waited for someone to tell us something. Mum told us what she knew about neck injury, which wasn't a lot. You could break the bones of your spine and be completely okay, she said, but what mattered was your spinal column. If that was damaged, that's when paralysis happened. So all we could do was wait, and try not to imagine the worst. That wasn't so easy. Emma was as pale as death and she chewed strands of her hair. We couldn't watch TV; we turned off the radio. Outside, the sky darkened and rain splodged the windows. Then it became more insistent; a wind picked up and hurled it against the glass, like a wild thing trying to get in. We watched it, mesmerised.

Mum was in command, trying to be resourceful. 'I'll ring the hospital,' she said. 'Now where would he be? At Brier Hall, or the District General?'

Brier Hall was the children's hospital. I was there when I broke my arm some years ago. It's just a kids' place, full of teddies and jigsaws and nursery rhyme posters on the wall. Bizarre to think of Simon there. The District General was the main hospital, where the A & E was. That was where Mum rang. She put on her most official voice, but all she managed to find out was that Simon had been admitted, and that the doctors were with him now, and no, they couldn't give out any information to general enquirers. 'No point ringing school,' Mum said unnecessarily, as it was a Saturday and none of us knew the teachers' private numbers.

So we waited. And waited. I got up and switched on the light as it was so dark outside. Three o'clock. Four o'clock. Dad passed by me and ruffled my hair. The cat came in, sat in the middle of the floor and proceeded to wash herself. We all watched her. I remembered about the match on TV that afternoon and found I didn't care who won any more. I looked at the clock again. Dad said I should take Emma for a walk, but we refused, we wouldn't leave the house. Mum made some sandwiches but we left them. Only David and Katy behaved normally, going upstairs to do something on the computer. We all tried pretending to them that nothing serious had happened to Simon, because it made us feel better. When we smiled at them, for a moment we believed our own lies.

Then the phone rang. We all looked at each other. Mum

answered. But it was only Wilko. He'd heard what had happened and had rung me for details. There was a rumour that Simon was dead. I put him right and then for the first time wondered if Simon might die. My skin turned icy with fear. I couldn't deal with the thought of him dying. Anyway, that wasn't going to happen. He was in the hospital, they'd look after him there, they'd make him better.

And we waited. I was glancing at the papers, Emma was staring out of the window. Then Mum shot out of her chair. 'Why didn't I think of it before? I'll ring Sylvia's sister! She'll know something.'

Mum chose to make the call upstairs – I think she needed the space. Those ten minutes were the hardest part. I took Emma's hand and squeezed it. The cat jumped up on her lap and pawed her legs. We heard Mum's footsteps slowly descending the stairs. It was the fact she was walking slowly – I knew it was bad news.

She came into the kitchen, glanced at Dad for support, avoided Emma, and looked directly at me. Her eyes said be strong. So I braced myself.

'There is news,' she said. She drew a deep breath. 'Simon's broken one of his cervical vertebrae and dislocated another. They say there is damage to the spinal cord, but' – she breathed hard again, and swallowed – 'but the swelling means they can't tell for sure . . . they can't see the whole extent. They're going to move him as soon as they can to a specialist spinal unit. They're saying' – another deep breath – 'they're saying to be prepared. It's unlikely he'll be able to walk again. It's a complete injury. From the chest down, there's no sensation, or movement . . .' My mum bit her lip hard and she was trembling.

I was numb with horror. I couldn't breathe, couldn't think, I didn't know what to do or say. At that moment the world stopped moving forward.

Me, Emma, all of us. We were paralysed.

SIMON

The flowers on the curtains are moving. They're having a war. They've knotted themselves together and now they're struggling to prise themselves apart. Look – a bunch of them have freed themselves and they've left the curtain and they're coming towards me. No, they're not flowers – it's a spinning grey blur with the letters GILBERT. The same as the letters on the rugby ball.

There's a pain somewhere. It's floating above me. It's not coming any closer but it's not going away either. I can't quite work out what I'm doing here. People are coming and going and they put me on this bed. I think something terrible must have happened to someone. Is this a film?

There's Emma. She's smiling at me. She wants to tell me something very important but her face has changed now and she's a lot older and her hair is blonde. I try to explain about the flowers on the curtain. I also want to ask what's happened but it's too hard to say what I mean. I don't like the way everything is moving around me. The ceiling is getting closer. There's a pain cloud over my head and it's trying to get in.

The light above me has detached itself from the ceiling

because it isn't a light, it's a flying saucer. It's landing on my bed and out come the flowers, who dance back to the curtains. I can hear the clatter of a trolley and someone calling and I think I might be in a hospital, but that doesn't make sense, and I guess that I'm dreaming, so I try to wake up. I think maybe a person is here with me but when I try to talk to them the words are thick and sticky in my mouth. I have to explain about the flowers.

Something is very wrong. I want to wake up.

I'm awake now. There's a light above my bed. It turns into a flying saucer. I knew it was going to do that. It's happened before. I'm stuck and everything is repeating itself. I want to get out of the loop. I'm scared shitless.

Here's my mum and dad. They look weird and anxious. I want to know what the time is. I try to ask them. They've gone dark and out of focus. Now here's someone else. They're turning me. Why can't I move my body? I don't understand this. But now, like a huge, dark wave, I can feel sleep coming. If I sleep, I'll wake up and feel better. I want to sleep. Sleep is stroking me with warm, velvet fingers and I'm going with her. I'm sinking down and down.

EMMA

I had a dream in which I was in a strange room, but with my mum and Steph. Mum was taking something out of a bag and I thought it might be a present for me. The feeling in the dream was warm and exciting at the same time. So when I woke up, on Monday morning, it was with a feeling of pleasure, and then . . . then . . . I remembered everything and it was as bad as it had ever been. No, worse. It was like it happened all over again in a moment.

Simon might never walk again. That's what they were saying. He was in hospital and they wouldn't let me see him because they were giving him morphine for the pain. I said to my mum, 'But how can he feel pain if he's paralysed?' And she said that his whole body was in shock. But he was lucky – *lucky!* – there was no brain damage, no complications, no need for surgery. But the doctors had said that the X-rays and scans showed there was damage to the spinal cord. And until the swelling subsided they couldn't really say how much. But they told us all to expect the worst. They were going to see if they could get him put straight into a specialist unit. And he would be there for a long time.

I lay in bed while tears squeezed themselves through my shut eyes and dampened the pillow. This was the cruellest, bleakest morning I had ever lived through. Everything seemed worse, not better. All of yesterday I was weepy and nothing my mum could do or say would cheer me up. I couldn't eat and every time the phone rang I jumped again in case it was Simon or news about Simon. Mum took the day off work – she's the manager of the fashion floor in Debenham's. She said she'd take me out and buy me something, but I didn't want to go. I know she was trying to cheer me up, but what was the point of looking good now? There was no Simon. Well, there is Simon, I know, but . . .

I cried some more. Mum heard me, came into my room, hugged me, then opened the curtains a little. I told her I didn't want to go to school but she insisted it was the best place for me, to be with my friends. In a way, I could see her point. So I got up and went through the motions: washing, dressing, dragging my unwashed hair back into a ponytail, sipping at some warm tea and refusing food. The idea of eating was impossible. I felt like my whole body had shut down. There was just a pricking pain pressing on my temples. Mum said I was still in shock. I guess she was right.

She also said I should try not to think about Simon, to give myself a break. But that was impossible. Every so often, like a newsflash interrupting a broadcast, pictures of Simon on the rugby field blotted out everything. I saw him leap for the ball, saw the other boy smash into him, watched Simon tumble in slow motion – and then I'd think: this whole hospital thing is a big mistake. He only fell onto the grass, for heaven's sake. He'll be fine. Everyone is over-reacting. I'll wake up in a minute and it will all have been a nightmare. Then reality would slap me in the face and it was like the whole thing was happening all over again. I just didn't know how I was going to cope.

All the way to school, I kept my head down. I wasn't ready to talk to anyone yet. It was hard to see the world carrying on as normal, as if what Simon was going through didn't matter. I heard some Year Nine girls giggling and a few Year Seven boys were chasing each other along the road. Obviously they didn't know what had happened yet. When it got around about Simon I reckoned the whole school would be stopped in its tracks. But now there was sunshine, kids chatting and playing – I felt like no one cared about us. People were going into school worrying about Physics tests or a boy who didn't text them. I'd never realised before how meaningless life really was.

Walking along the corridor to the Sixth Form centre was the hardest part. Normally I had my eyes peeled for Simon, or he'd be lounging by the chocolate machine pretending not to wait for me, but, of course, he was. Then, for one crazy split-second, I thought I saw him. Someone was standing there – it was a boy, but then whoever it was moved away, leaving a vacuum. How dare he stand there? It wasn't fair. Tears sprung to my eyes again but this time I bit my lip hard to stop them. The last thing I wanted was to walk into the Sixth Form centre sobbing my heart out. I didn't want sympathy. It was Simon who needed it, not me.

The room was deathly quiet. Although most of our year was there, the radio wasn't playing. People were standing around in knots and I knew they were all talking about Simon. He was public property. And when people saw me, the silence deepened. I knew what they were thinking: Emma's boyfriend is paralysed. How's she reacting? It was awful, feeling so exposed and so pitied.

In a moment Steph was at my side and hugging me. I did cry then, gently, making a damp patch on her shoulder. Jen came over too and some of the other girls. I could see a lot of them had been crying too. That made me feel worse, somehow. It was proof of the enormity of Simon's accident. They sat me down and Steph wouldn't let go of me, she kept my hand tight in hers. Wilko came over. He said, 'I'm sorry, Em.' I just nodded, I couldn't look at him.

Everything was wrong, horrible and ugly. The blue chairs looked garish and random, the posters on the wall were crass and pointless, lockers were open exposing untidy piles of books and folders. No sense or meaning anywhere.

Julia came over – I don't know her very well, she's in another class.

'How are you, Emma? How are you feeling?'

'Leave her alone,' Jen said. 'Push off.'

She backed away. 'I was only asking how she was. Honestly!'

I could feel Jen trying to protect me and I was grateful. Grateful too, for Steph's solid presence. Jen shooed people away, and Steph started talking.

'How bad is he? Do you know?'

'He has to have tests,' I said. 'But the doctors told his mum and dad he probably won't walk again.'

'How do they know?' Steph questioned eagerly.

'Because they're doctors,' I said.

'Doctors don't know everything. They can get things wrong. I should know – remember my mum is a nurse! The thing about doctors, Emma, they always tell you the worst. They have to, so they don't turn out to be wrong.'

'They tell you the worst?'

'Yeah, absolutely. Because all the time they're dealing with very ill people, they just always see the worst-case scenario. So Simon is admitted to the hospital and they're like, he'll never walk again. But he might. Even you said he hasn't had all the tests yet.'

I was silent, listening intently.

'At this specialist unit, they'll have a much better idea. Did you know something like this happened to the daughter of a friend of my mum's? She came off her bike and when she tried to get up, she couldn't feel a thing. They rushed her off to hospital but bit by bit she got sensation back. She was back at home in three days.'

'Really?'

'Yes, because when you injure your spine, it all swells up. They call it spinal shock – my mum explained all this. And until the swelling goes down they can't really be sure about anything. So you mustn't give up hope, honestly, Emma. And even if Simon can't walk for a bit, they're always discovering new things, new ways of curing people who used to be incurable. Who's to say they won't pioneer some new treatment specially for him?'

I squeezed her hand as tight as I could. I loved no one in the world more than Steph at that moment. She had given me Simon back, she had given me my life back.

'Hey, Emma, in a few weeks' time, you'll be visiting him in hospital and he'll be walking towards you on crutches. Just imagine that. The more you imagine it, the more it might happen.'

'You're right,' I whispered. 'It would be wrong of me to give up hope.'

'Si would want you to believe in him,' she told me.

I just nodded, my heart full. Simon was going to get better. And I was going to help him, by not giving in to despair. I was going to be brave and keep my head up high. Steph was completely right. Why accept the doctors' gloomy predictions? Miracles *do* happen. I could see a light at the end of my tunnel and it was getting bigger and brighter with every second.

So I looked up, swallowed my tears and attempted a

smile. And at that moment Danny came into the centre. His face was black as thunder. Adam came up to him but Danny pushed him away. He just went to his locker and stood there with his back to everyone. I saw people wonder what to do. You could tell his mates wanted to support him, but he was sending off signals saying, don't go anywhere near me, just leave me alone.

The school bell rang. Normally we all pile into assembly but before we had a chance to move, Mr Neale appeared. He told us to stay where we were, because we were going to have a separate gathering. We all knew why.

But I was feeling different now. Steph had set my mind moving in another direction entirely. Simon was going to make a complete recovery – and I would help him do it. You see, the misery I was feeling, the way my world had collapsed, *that* was the bit that couldn't be true. Like in a film, there are scenes you can't bear to watch, and you hide your face in your hands; but when you open your eyes, the action's moved on, it's daylight and children are laughing. There's going to be a happy ending.

I cast another glance at Danny and I became convinced that it wasn't just Simon that caused that expression on his face. Something else had happened. Something that had made him not sad, but angry. So angry that he wasn't really sure how to deal with his anger. Then I thought: I'll talk to him. Steph had made me feel so much better and I decided to pass that feeling on.

As we all quietened down to listen to Mr Neale, I whispered to Steph, 'I'll never forget what you just said. You've helped me loads. I'm so lucky to have a friend like you.' I saw her wipe away a tear.

Mr Neale began. 'As you all know, Simon Denham was injured in Saturday's rugby match. I think it's important we gather together this morning, away from the main school, so I can give you a clear picture of how he is, to prevent the spreading of any rumours.'

He was calm, but he looked as if he was finding it hard to speak to us. He gave an account of the accident. He said that it was Simon's utter determination to get the ball that meant he didn't see his opposite number was going for it too. He told everyone what I already knew – that Simon would be transferred to a specialist unit and that he wasn't allowed any visitors.

'His life is *not* in danger,' he said emphatically. 'However, it is very unlikely he will walk again and possible that he will have only limited arm movement too.'

No! I found myself silently screaming, blocking out his voice. It *is* likely he will walk again – just you wait. Mr Neale, all the teachers and parents and everybody, they're old – what do they know about hope? They always take the dimmest view. I *know* Simon will get better.

'I also want to make it very clear that the boy who collided with him was in no way to blame. No one was to blame for what happened to Simon. He was very, very unlucky. The Head is speaking to the rest of school in main assembly. Now we will have a moment's silence for reflection. Those of you who wish to pray, may do so.'

Silence. '*Dear God*,' I thought. I know that's not how you start a prayer, but I wanted to get straight to the point. '*Make him better soon*.' Then I stopped. I thought of what Steph said: here comes Simon, walking towards me on crutches – no, not on crutches – he flings them away, I run to him, and he folds me in his arms.

DANNY

'No one was to blame for what happened to Simon. He was very, very unlucky. The Head is speaking to the rest of the school in main assembly. Now we will have a moment's silence . . .'

No one was to blame for what happened to Simon. I knew better. It was that knowledge that was eating away at me. Within about thirty minutes of hearing about his accident, I realised who had done it. But just like the worst sort of guilty criminal, the skulking, sneaking, low sort of scum who never admits to anything, I wasn't going to tell.

Simon had said we'd go to town on Saturday, talk about what Mr Neale had said. I'd said, sure. And then the party had gone on, and I'd been drinking, and the idea of getting up early on Saturday morning was a pain, so I'd postponed to Sunday afternoon. So when the call came for Simon to substitute, he was free. If I hadn't broken the arrangement, he'd have been committed to me, and this nightmare morning at school would never have happened. Simon never broke a promise, ever. He wouldn't have played in that match if it wasn't for my idleness, the same idleness that Neale and my parents were on at me to tackle. Too late. Too damn late.

I told no one that. Instead I told it to myself, over and over and again, lacerating myself with the knowledge *I'd* done it, I'd crippled my best mate. I made myself imagine Simon crumpling into a heap on the pitch – and it was me, just me, who'd put him there. The worse I made myself feel, the better it was. I needed to make myself suffer.

When assembly had finished, some people tried slapping me on the back, saying stuff, offering condolences, but I didn't deserve them. I couldn't bear anyone around me. I saw Mr Neale approach me, his eyes seeking mine; but I avoided him and I noticed his momentary hesitation – I saw he was unsure what to do, or what to say to me. Everyone thought I was acting like this because I was upset. Which was true, I was upset, but it was a whole lot worse than that.

I sat at the back of the English room, put a file on my desk, but I didn't have the poetry anthology with me. Emma came to sit by me but I didn't acknowledge her. I'd ruined her life too. I noticed she didn't look too bad. Her face was kind of . . . lit up, like she could see something we couldn't. It was easy for her to be brave – she was innocent.

The lesson began and the teacher's words echoed around the room. She hadn't acknowledged Simon and I thought she was callous. I was also glad she hadn't. I didn't listen to a thing she said after that. She could have been talking in another language. Emma occasionally wrote something down. I glanced at her anthology but the poem didn't make any sense to me, nor did I want it to.

I wondered what Simon was doing. What did you do when you'd broken your back? Just lie there. They said he was under sedation. No visitors, they said. I was relieved. How could I face him? The biggest irony: here was I, prize slob Danny Harrison, with a fully working body, and Simon, school hero, lying there useless, for ever. Maybe on some deep level I wanted this to happen – who knows? I was scum, complete and utter scum. I buried my head in my arms on the desk, I didn't care who saw.

'Danny?' Emma whispered. She touched my back lightly. 'You okay? Do you want to leave the lesson?'

'Shove off,' I said.

I squeezed my eyes tight shut to blot out everything, until all I could see were swirls and flashes.

'Danny,' came the teacher's voice. 'Is there anything I can do?' I didn't move. I could feel the concentrated attention of the class pressing on me. I felt myself pushing it away. They left me alone.

At break I went to sit in the library. The people I saw shot me odd looks. I'd been so successful in deflecting attention I'd frightened everyone off. Good. Exactly what I deserved. I took a magazine from the rack but didn't open it. Instead I replayed again what I'd said to Simon. 'Ten tomorrow morning? Way too early. I'll call in the afternoon.' So I'd freed him to throw his life away.

I didn't move from my seat in the library. There was no point going to any more lessons. The librarian asked me if I wanted anything – everyone was so damn solicitous, so polite. They had no idea who they were talking to.

Lunchtime, I continued to sit there. I liked the dead books on the shelves, the weight of the words still on the pages. The old books that no one ever read, dead. Then Emma came.

'Danny, I've been looking for you everywhere!'

I grunted.

'We're going out. Just up the road a while.' She tugged at my arm and I resisted her pull. Then I noticed some kids were staring and I felt a bit of a fool. I had no choice but to get up.

'That's better,' she said. She led me down the corridor and out of a door. She marched me along the road. The fresh air was a relief. Her step was quick and determined and I increased my pace to keep up with her. We didn't speak. I noticed people's curious glances. I was under no illusions, I knew what people were thinking: there goes the girlfriend and the best mate of that boy who was paralysed. Ghouls, gawping.

We walked until we were well away from school. The avenue we were in was lined with barren trees, leaves shed ready for winter. Emma found a bench and stood by it, waiting for me to sit. I did. I could feel her will was stronger than mine.

She sat by me. A beat, and then, 'He's going to get better, you know.'

I raised my head. 'Who told you?' At the prospect, a dawning light illuminated my blackness.

'I know,' she said simply. 'I just know it.'

The light sputtered, and went out.

'The specialists haven't examined him yet and they'll see things differently. They'll know what can be done. And can you imagine Simon just giving in? And all the time they're finding new treatments. Steph said, and her mother's a nurse.'

Steph said. Steph, who can't bear anyone to be unhappy for a moment. She'd sell her grandmother to put a smile on your face. I could see it all. She'd been filling Emma full of false hope, just to make her feel better. And it had worked. But my parents had been completely on the level with me. Simon's spinal cord was damaged. No one has discovered a way of repairing damaged spinal cords. Otherwise Christopher Reeve would have been back playing Superman. So I just nodded without meeting her eyes. If living in cloud cuckoo land was going to help Emma, I wasn't going to tell it like it is. I'd already done enough harm.

'So cheer up, Danny,' she said. 'As soon as he's allowed visitors, you and me will go together and bring him lots of pressies.'

No, I wasn't ready for that yet. I shook my head.

'Why not?' she asked. 'Don't you like hospitals?'

I don't, but that wasn't the reason. So I shrugged.

'Danny!' Emma exclaimed. 'Speak to me! It's not going to help Simon, you being in the pits like this.'

I felt even more guilty.

'Honestly, Dan, you're acting as if *you* did it!'

I quickly turned my head away. Emma caught the movement.

'Danny? I don't get this. You were nowhere around when the accident happened.'

'That,' I said, 'is the bloody point.'

Once I explained, Emma would never be able to speak to me again.

'I'm sorry. You've lost me completely.'

I muttered, 'Simon should have been in town with me.'

Emma was still for a moment or two. An elderly man in a flat cap walked past us. Some pigeons settled nearby and strutted importantly.

'Oh!' Emma said. 'You mean Simon had arranged to meet you and then when we said goodbye you postponed him. I was there. I remember.'

One pigeon chased another away, its hooded head like a little piston. I waited for Emma's anger and disgust to pour out over me.

'So you feel guilty! I see it. No, Danny, it's not your fault at all.'

Yeah, right.

'Then it's his parents' fault for driving him to the match, Mr Smith's for ringing him, mine for not demanding that he see me instead, the boy who collided with him, the boy who kicked the ball he went for – Danny, it's everybody's fault. It's nobody's fault.'

I heard what she said and admitted she made some kind of sense. But what she said didn't ring true. I still felt as if I had caused the accident. I knew it shouldn't be me sitting on this bench with Emma, but Simon. My burden of guilt redistributed itself, but didn't go away.

'You can't think like that,' Emma said. 'It's not helping anyone. What we ought to be doing is working out ways to support Simon. When he gets back to school he'll probably still be a bit shaky on his legs, and he'll need you to go around with him and make sure the little kids don't knock him over.' She nudged me in a friendly way. 'Cheer up, Danny,' she said. 'Your best mate needs you.'

For Emma's sake, I attempted a smile.

'Me and Steph, we're planning his welcome home party. Don't think he'll be up to dancing, but then he was never very good on the club floor.'

What was she on about? Didn't she realise how serious it was? Simon was going to need a wheelchair. Right now he had no feeling in any part of his lower body and might never again. He might not even be able to use his arms – they would have to wait and see.

My guilt dispersed for now, but only because I realised that Emma was in a worse state. She was in complete denial. She sat by my side, her face pale and her eyes alight. Emma wanted to be an actor – she'd starred in a number of school productions. Now, I reckoned, she had embarked upon the performance of a lifetime. She was the star and audience both. She'd utterly convinced herself.

And who was I to tell her she was living a dream?

SIMON

It might be the morning. I'm not sure because the lights are still dimmed. I can't see the window from where my bed is. My eyes are trained on the ceiling. When it's brighter I watch the hairline crack above me meandering along like the snaking bends of a river. Once I spotted a very small insect that landed by it and then shot off. Just now is one of the easier times. I'm in discomfort, not pain, and I think that soon one of the nurses will come and move me. I think it's nearly time.

They tell me they have to do that because of the pressure sores. I can't lie in one position all of the time. So they come and have a chat and gently push me into a slightly different posture, firming up the cushions. I still can't feel anything – but that's the spinal shock. The whole system freezes, so there's no sensation at all. I feel like half a person. I can't even move the top half of my body because of the halo traction.

They did that shortly after I came here, to this unit. I lay on this bed and they all stood over me, and gave me a local anaesthetic, and explained they were going to drill small holes just above my ears. I tried to act brave. Then they fixed the halo – the semi-circular bar that's joined to my head – and I felt my head tilt back as they attached weights to it. The weights are lying behind me, on the floor, and that's why my head is fixed at this angle, my eyes staring up. This is to correct the dislocation, instead of surgery. So I can't move my head at all. I can't even turn to look at the curtains around my bed. I'm not even sure what my ward looks like, or how many other beds are here. But to be honest, for a lot of the time I don't care. There's so much else to think about.

But there's also nothing to think about, except: I must get better. I know I've broken my C7 cervical vertebra and dislocated my C6. I've been in spinal shock. That's receding now and very soon they'll be able to tell exactly what's wrong. Maybe today. I hope so. They've told me I might not be able to walk. Well, okay, not in the beginning, I reckon not. But there's going to be rehab, I suppose, getting back to moving about, using a wheelchair in the first instance, then maybe crutches.

Time passes very slowly. I look forward to my visitors. At the moment these are just Mum and Dad. I saw David briefly but he wouldn't get close to me. I just glimpsed him and Dad shooed him away. Mum has been here most of all, every day, standing over me – unless she stands over me, I can't see her. She's fiercely protective; questions the doctors, the nurses; tries to interpret what they say to me and asks me what she can do to help me. She's also acting brave.

I know it's an act. She can't kid me. I saw the way she looked at me, the first time she saw me. Her eyes reflected her shock and horror. She didn't need to speak. I thought whatever is wrong with me must be very serious – and Dad, he just looked broken. I wanted them to go away and the normal, cheerful nurses to come back. But also I wanted them there all the time, so I wouldn't get swallowed up by this alien place.

I ask Mum about everyone else: Emma, Dan, my friends. But she doesn't know much except they send their regards. Except none of my mates would say that – that they send their regards. Those aren't the words they'd use. Mum says it's too early for me to have visitors other than family. She says once I've got rid of the halo traction, I'll look better. But how can I wait that long? The doctor said it could be a month, six weeks. And I want my friends more than anything. But on the other hand, I have to consider what Emma would think if she saw me like this. That I'm a freak. Mr Metal Man. So I agreed with my mum, and she's been reading me letters and cards from everyone. Emma says I have to be positive and she can't wait to see me. She said she loved me, and when my mum read that out she sounded a bit surprised. The class sent a card which everyone signed. There are flowers which I can't see, but sometimes a fresh, silky smell wafts over. Wilko sent a card saying keep your chin up – which made me smile, as with this halo traction I have no option but to keep my chin up!

And then there was Dan. He never sent a card, but a cassette tape which my mum played. He didn't spend too long with the good wishes or the soppy stuff, but just launched into all the gossip. And it was great. It was good to know who Jen was after now and that Mr Neale wouldn't let Wilko drop Philosophy and Ethics because he didn't understand it. He gave me a blow-by-blow account of the football. He recorded a new track of a band we both like. I got the nurses to play that to me over and over. If there's one person I want to see, it's Dan. I decide to ask Mum if he could be allowed to come.

But hearing Danny going on about our crowd and our lives also made me feel worse. I'm no longer part of them. Will they forget about me? Of course I know they'll visit me and be there for me and all of that rubbish – but their real lives will carry on without me. I wonder will I ever get back to how I was? And will I play rugby again?

I lie here and think these things, over and over again. I can't imagine a life without rugby. It's what I do – it's who I am. But in a year, say – I want to be realistic here – maybe I can be back on the field, though I accept it'll be some time before I'll be as good as I was. I think about rugby a lot. Playing imaginary games in my mind helps me to focus, to forget where I am. Sometimes I try to remember my accident. The game started, and I tackled the centre, received a miss pass, releasing the inside centre who'd looped, then there was a scrum – then it's as if a camera inside my head jams and I remember nothing. It's all an absolute blank. The only pictures I have are the ones other people have given me: you jumped for the ball, you collided with Rob Smith from Millbank College, you smashed onto the ground and lay there – and I can't honestly say whether it's true or not. I have no choice but to believe them. Only deep down I don't understand how rugby, which I love so much, could have done this to me.

While I lie here, I worry too – and not just about me. One of the worst things about being here in this state is what it's doing to the family. I feel I've let them down. Only here's another contradiction. Trying so hard to get that ball – that was part of what I was doing for Mum and Dad. I love being able to tell them what I've achieved, and the look on their faces: pride, pleasure – and just for a moment our family is whole, complete, perfect. And now I've made a bigger mess than ever, bigger than my dad; I've brought everything crashing down around me.

Part of me says, *don't think like that*. It says, *you've got to be positive. Get better, get back, and everything will be just as it was*. Maybe I can make a success of my recovery. That thought pleases me, and I make myself have it as much as possible. I think it when the gross things happen: the catheter, the drip, when the nurses do stuff to me so I can empty my bowels – I just blank it all out and think: I'm going to put up with all of this, better than anyone thinks I will.

I try to give all this thinking a rest. I'm fed up with the way my thoughts go round in circles. I try to listen to the noises outside and work out what's happening. Maybe a nurse will come soon – I hope so. I get fed up with all this waiting.

Then I tell myself: waiting is hard, but it's what I have to do. Lots of it, they say. And I will, because I can still think and breathe and talk – I'm still alive. There's a feeling strong inside me, like a flame, which is going to make the best of this and get me out of here. I have to work hard at getting better. That's what I have to do. And the way I must work hard is by doing nothing.

And then the nurses come in and there's one of the doctors with them. The nurses check my drip and begin to move me. The doctor asks me how I'm feeling and I say I'm fine. He asks if my mother is around and I tell him that she's coming a bit later on. I ask why. He hesitates – and I know immediately what's up. He has some news: he's been able to assess the damage.

He confirms that, and says it can wait. I might prefer to have my parents with me when I hear.

'No,' I say, swiftly and emphatically. Because already I knew from his tone: soft, concerned, serious. It was bad news. My heart starts racing and I feel sweat on my forehead. But I prefer to hear it now, from him, like an adult. I don't want to have to cope with my mum's reaction as well. So I insist he tells me. He looks uneasy. He comes and stands over me and I look up into his face. A neat beard, glasses – I can see his nostrils, small and dark.

'As you know, Simon, your spinal cord has sustained damage. The spinal cord is an extension of the brain, it's the way the brain controls the body, and if part of it is injured, it's like a computer system crashing and no messages are getting sent out. That's why you can't feel anything or move anything.'

Yeah, yeah, I thought, get on with it.

'But there is a difference. You can get a computer system up and running again. But the spinal cord can't regenerate itself. Any damage is permanent.'

Permanent?

'You won't walk again,' he said. 'The movement in your hands will be affected too. You'll get better than you are now, depending on how your rehabilitation goes. But you mustn't expect to walk again.'

I say, 'I know I won't for quite a while . . .'

'Never, Simon.'

A nurse chips in. 'It's better for you to know this now,' she says, and places her cool hand on my damp forehead. Panic swells in my chest.

'But can't I try?' I hear myself saying.

'There's lots you can still do in a wheelchair,' the doctor tells me.

'But what about . . .?'

He seems to read my mind.

'We'll show you ways of managing bladder and bowel control. You'll find different ways of doing all the things you used to do.'

His words weren't going in. Not walking. Not running. Never being on the rugby field again. And Emma – how can you kiss a girl from a wheelchair? And the rest – we were supposed to be having sex. And what did he mean by bladder and bowel control? That I couldn't piss or shit normally again? Or get a hard-on? I'm reeling from this, I'm not able to accept it.

'No,' I said. 'You're wrong. I will get better.'

'You will,' said the doctor. 'You'll be much better than you are now. But you won't be the same. I know you think I'm being harsh and I give you permission to hate me for a while. But you need to accept the condition you're in. It's a vital part of your recovery.'

I am more frightened than I have ever been. I can't believe that all my life has been taken away from me. And it really feels like that. If I can't ever walk, *ever*, then who am I? What will I become? This is worse than dying.

They all stay with me, but I don't really hear what they're saying. I can't take it all in. I am utterly devastated.

Then a strange thing happens. The fear ebbs away. The fact remains. I'm paralysed. I accept it. In this here and now, I am in a spinal unit on halo traction and although one day I'll get out of here, it'll be in a wheelchair. That's the bottom line. I can handle it. Why? Because I have no choice.

The nurse says something about me being brave and the doctor asks if he should speak to my parents, or would I like to tell them? I say he can explain everything. I don't mind. I don't care. I want them all to go and leave me. In time, they do.

I'm alone again and struggling to accept what I've just heard. Part of me still doesn't believe them and wants to prove them wrong. But the rest of me knows the truth, and maybe always has done.

From now on, I'm a cripple. And I'm just going to have to learn to cope with it. I remember what the doctor said – there'll be different ways of doing things. I'll just have to learn them all. I'm going to see this through. I'm going to be strong. Really strong.

I feel a tear trickle down one side of my face.

DANNY

There's nothing worse than being the centre of attention at school because your best mate's lying useless in hospital. Correction: there is. It's when you stop being the centre of attention. Three weeks on, the school had got used to the situation with Simon. Kids no longer gave me sympathetic glances. Not everyone came over in the morning to ask, 'Any more news?' After three weeks, it was business as usual.

Business as usual for them, maybe. But me and Emma – we were still waiting to see him. Simon had been moved to the spinal unit and we were told it was family only visiting. So twelve-year-old David had been to see him, but not us, which is crazy. Last night David had tea with us. He was sitting there putting numbers into his new phone. It was just a toy for him and he wanted as many numbers as possible. So I let him have mine and Emma's. After a while I interrupted him and asked what it was like visiting Simon. He shrugged and said, 'All right.' Mum shot me a warning glance and I backed off.

Later when Sylvia and John came to pick him up, I asked again, 'When can I visit?' John said, 'At the weekend,' and again there was a series of coded glances between parents as if I was some sort of retard who couldn't be trusted in a hospital. I said I'd bring Emma and as I mentioned her name the atmosphere became even more tense. I couldn't quite work out what was going on. I didn't understand why John and Sylvia were so reluctant to let us see Simon. Maybe Emma would find it hard, granted, but not me.

I was glad when John and Sylvia left. It wasn't that I don't like them, I do – kind of. Sylvia's a very full-on sort of mum, in that she's always fussing round you. John doesn't say a great deal. No, to be honest, something else was bugging me. I was wondering how they felt seeing me still walking, still fit and well. I couldn't rid myself of the feeling it should have been me.

So I was focussing on my first visit to Simon. That was my reality and school was just a charade I had to get through. I was only turning up each day because it was better than sitting at home. No other reason. I couldn't be bothered with lessons, not at all. So that Friday I decided to skip Politics and hide out somewhere no one would think of looking for me. I thought of the library. Sorted.

I found an easy chair near the senior fiction and settled down. I adjusted the earphone of my Walkman so no one could see it from a distance. Once I'd seen Simon, I guessed I would feel better. I tried to think what he must be going through, just lying there. What do you think about when you can't move, when nurses have to do everything for you, when you know you're never going to walk again?

After about half an hour a teacher came in with a load of Year Sevens. She explained to them about the library classification system and gave them some questions so they could find stuff out. I saw her casting meaningful looks in my direction. But she didn't come over to me.

One of the class did, though. A fat kid with specs and hamster cheeks. He stared at me like I was a prize exhibit at a freak show.

'Are you the friend of that boy who's paralysed?'

'Yeah,' I said. 'Now fuck off.'

Sorry, it slipped out. I was curious to see what the kid would do. Tell the teacher, probably. But he just stood there. He said, 'Give him my best wishes,' and wandered away.

I felt like vermin again. The kid wasn't being nosy. He wanted to do the decent thing. Why was it I couldn't get anything right? I felt my face contort with self-loathing.

After a while, the class went. I saw that teacher look at me again. I didn't know who she was. Our school is pretty big – it's an eleven-to-eighteen independent mixed school. Teachers come and go.

Ten minutes later, Mr Neale came in. I realised that other teacher had been checking on me. Here we go. Time for him to read out the riot act. Neale is a big guy, over six foot. He crouched down beside me.

'Shouldn't you be in Politics?'

Daft question. But I conceded an answer. ' 'Spose.'

'Don't think you'd be better off in lessons?'

The question was a trap. If I said yes, I'd sound a right idiot. If I said no, I'd be defying him. Mr Neale had it in for me. He always has done, from the start. My guess was he'd have liked me out of the school. I remained silent. I heard Mr Neale draw a deep breath.

'Simon wouldn't want you moping like this.'

I filled with incandescent rage. How the hell did *he* know what Simon was thinking? If anyone knew, I did. He was a cripple, his life in ruins. He'd want me to mourn with him. How would he feel if he knew I was just carrying on as usual, without a care in the world? My face betrayed my anger. Mr Neale got to his feet.

'Come to my office, Daniel.'

I didn't meet his eyes but got up, took the earphone out of my ear, picked up my bag and followed him out of the library, past the corridor with all the artwork on it, round the corner and through the IT resource centre to his room. He indicated the chair in front of his desk and I sat there. He didn't go and sit behind his desk but carried on standing, scowling down at me from a great height.

'I know how you feel,' he said.

I could have laughed at that.

'But by opting out like this you're not going to improve the situation for anyone. I've been watching you since the accident and I didn't want to come down too heavily on you at the beginning. But for your own sake, lad, pull yourself together.'

The truth was, I wanted to hit him. My fists were tingling. He didn't have any idea what I was going through, or what Simon was going through. The anger gathered force like a tidal wave, then crashed and poured through me, spilling itself uselessly.

'Remember you're on report,' he said.

I raised my eyebrows and half-smiled at him. Did he honestly believe my report meant anything to me now? He took another deep breath. It amused and scared me to see he really didn't know how to handle me. He had met his match.

'Danny, would you like to see a counsellor?'

This time I said, 'And a counsellor would help Simon to walk again?'

'No, but maybe talking would help you come to terms with it.'

Yeah. Like Emma, who was constantly surrounded by girls, talking and talking and talking and persuading themselves that a miracle would happen. Talking and crying and hugging each other, enjoying it, it seemed to me, getting a kick out of the whole thing. I looked up at Mr Neale and my eyes said no. Talking solved nothing. I knew it and he knew it.

Mr Neale wiped his forehead with the back of his hand. Yep, he was finding this tough.

'Okay, Danny,' he said. 'I want you to go back to lessons. As of now. I'm formally reminding you that you're on report.

Failure to hand in work set will result in your parents being called in, and if there's no subsequent improvement, we'll have to discuss your future plans.'

Which was a euphemism for kicking me out. Would you believe it? My best mate crippled and the Head of Sixth giving me an ultimatum. That's the kind of man Neale was. Standing there in a suit and flashy tie, on a power trip. His face was set, stern and tight. No sympathy there at all.

'Yeah, whatever,' I mumbled.

I decided I'd go back to lessons for now. As for working, we'd see. I felt a mild panic tingle through me. It was true I hadn't been handing in essays and I didn't fully know why. It started way before Simon's accident. I just couldn't be bothered a lot of the time. Even at GCSE I left all my revision to the last minute and, after results, I had to see the Head about my under-performance and I had to sign all sorts of papers about using study periods to study and not hang around in the Sixth Form centre. I meant to change my ways, but the work was boring, and I felt myself falling behind, and some of the teachers had it in for me. And it was probably true that my behaviour wasn't up to much – I like a laugh, that's all. But I didn't want to leave school. It's where all my mates are. Were.

'Have you been to visit Simon yet?' he asked suddenly.

I shook my head, then mumbled, 'Tomorrow.'

'Give him my best wishes. If he's up for visitors, I'll pop in myself. He's at the unit in Southfields, isn't he?'

I smiled for the first time. Imagine Simon's face when Neale turns up!

'I know the hospital,' he said.

The bell went. Mr Neale consulted his watch. 'Break now. Then . . .' he looked at some papers on his desk. On the top was my personal timetable. 'English for you. I'll pop my head in and give you a friendly wave.'

Why do teachers think it's so clever to do the good cop/bad cop routine? I got to my feet, picked up my bag and left the office. The funny thing was, as I made my way to the Sixth Form centre, I found I was feeling a little better. I didn't know why.

EMMA

Danny told me he didn't like hospitals much either. He reckoned it stemmed from the time he had to have stitches in A & E when he was six.

'You screamed all the time,' his dad commented from the driver's seat.

'It hurt!' Dan said.

I smiled. Everyone was being courageous, light-hearted. We turned into the hospital complex and tried to find the signs for the unit. The hospital was like a little town, a mixture of old and new buildings, and building works. There were car parks, one-way systems, and huge signposts listing all the different departments. As we turned corner after corner, I held the bag steady that contained all the cards and presents from people at school. On my lap was a bunch of roses from me to Simon, a box of chocolates and a framed photo of us together on the beach in the summer.

I felt apprehensive, it was true. Simon's mum warned me he had to lie down all the time and that he had drips and traction and things. Well, everyone did in hospital. I knew that. My mum said that seeing him would help me feel better. He would become a real person to me again. I knew I would have to make adjustments. I wasn't that naïve.

In amongst all my nervousness, though, I was really looking forward to seeing Simon. I had lots of encouraging things to tell him. Jen, who's whizz at IT, had been surfing the net, and she discovered they're pioneering a new treatment for spinal cord injuries with stem cell implants to repair the damage, and she read about a girl who was paralysed from the neck down and they said she'd never walk again and she did.

'That must be it,' Danny's mum said.

The unit was a modern building and I was pleased. Hospitals aren't so scary if they're modern – they look more like the hospitals on TV. We parked in a small car park and went over the arrangements again. Danny's parents said they'd let us go in by ourselves, but they'd come in later to say hello to Simon too. Danny said nothing. I could tell he was uneasy. He said to me, 'You all right, Em?'

'I'm fine,' I told him. 'You?'

'Whatever.'

We found the lobby where the lifts are, and a man in a wheelchair was waiting to go in too. When the lift arrived I was about to offer to push him in, but he zoomed in by himself and asked us where we wanted to go, then pressed the lift buttons, which were low down.

And there we were on the floor where the wards were.

There was a nurses' station in the middle, with a computer and office-y things. There were wards radiating off the central area. I thought how light and airy it all was. I realised I was right to be optimistic. Still, I was a little bit jumpy. I knew my pulse was racing. To encourage myself I thought that the last time I saw Simon he was lying crumpled on the rugby pitch – he was bound to look a lot better now. Danny's mum had a word with one of the nurses and she indicated one of the wards. Just then Simon's mum came out of the same one and we all said hello. They told us where he was – the bed on the left.

Danny took my hand – no, he *grabbed* my hand. I could see he was tense and I whispered to him to relax. I didn't want Simon to see us looking upset. But it's hard. When you're in a hospital, you're always scared of seeing something you don't want to. I kept my eyes focussed on what should be Simon's bed.

I couldn't take it all in at first. He was lying flat on it, staring at the ceiling, his face pulled back and his mouth open. And round his head was a black U-shape and – no, it was attached to his head . . . how did they do that? And a drip was stuck on his nose and there was stuff in it, a liquid. I felt my stomach heave. My legs gave way and I clung on to Danny. I wanted to run away. I just couldn't stay one more moment. I couldn't breathe properly and I was about to turn and go . . .

. . . and a voice in me, or outside me, said, *stay. You've got to remain here. What would Simon think if you turned and ran?* It was as if someone was telling me what to do, but that someone was me. I can't, I argued. I'll be sick. I'll cry or scream. *You'll be fine*, said the voice. *Stay for just a few minutes.*

Danny crossed past me and moved over to Simon's head.

'How you doing?' he said. I heard the catch in his voice.

'Not too bad.' Simon's voice was tiny, congested, not like him. 'I'm not allowed to move my head. Look under my bed. There are weights attached to this halo-thing.' Danny and I saw the weights. That was why his head was held at that strange angle. Then Simon said, 'Emma?'

I moved forward, my heart pounding in my chest. It repulsed me, the drip and the pins in his head. But I could still trace my Simon in that figure on the bed. I didn't know what to say. Again I wanted to run away. But Danny took my hand and put it on Simon's. Simon's hand moved under mine but he didn't seem to have much force or energy in it.

'Thanks for coming,' he said.

I was crying now – I couldn't help it.

'It's all right,' Simon said, in that strange voice.

'It's just . . . the shock,' I mumbled. 'I've got some presents for you.' I began to get things out of the bag: the cards, the chocolates. How was he going to eat them? I put the flowers on his bedside table. Doing things calmed me down.

When I looked at him again, it was a little easier. But I didn't like the drip. And then I saw a plastic bag attached to the side of the bed and there was a yellow liquid inside. I didn't want to think what that was. I moved up the bed and stood close to Simon's head again. I felt him looking up at me. Danny took a seat. My eyes were straying around the bed. I noticed the paraphernalia on his bedside table: a cassette player, cards, medical things. His bed had a metal frame, the sheets were white, there were pillows propping his body. Simon was dressed in a tracksuit with baggy trousers. I couldn't see his legs. I didn't want to. I could feel the panic mounting again.

I hadn't realised how ugly illness was. All the metal and tubes and drips were so impersonal and harsh. Simon was lying there like a prisoner, like someone in a torture chamber. I felt such huge pity for him. It swelled in my chest like a balloon and almost stopped me breathing.

Danny said, 'How did they fix that thing on your head, Si?'

'They drilled holes above my ears,' he said. And went on to explain exactly how they did it. I tried not to listen.

'Like Frankenstein,' Danny said, 'with that bolt through his neck.'

I saw Simon attempt a smile and I loved Danny for making him smile.

'Do you get bored?' Danny asked. 'And I'm not referring to the traction holes.'

The boys both laughed. They're so strange. How could they joke at a time like this?

Simon settled down. 'Yes and no. I . . . Time doesn't pass like it does normally. I get tired a lot of the time. And the drugs space me out.'

'What are you on?' Dan asked. 'Can I have some?'

'It'll cost you,' Simon said.

I was glad they were joking, but felt left out. Still my eyes were roving over the ward. There were alarms in case of an emergency. I saw a TV attached to a bracket high up on the wall so Simon could see it. I tried not to look at where the halo went into his head.

'When will you be sitting up?' Dan asked.

'Not for quite a few weeks, maybe even a couple of months.'

That shocked me. Danny was quiet for a moment, which gave me a chance. I moved back to Simon's head, and smiled down at him.

'And when will you be walking again?'

'I won't,' he said to me.

'You will,' I said. I repeated what Jen had told me.

'No, Emma,' Simon said. His eyes slid from mine. 'The doctor said it's certain I won't regain any real movement. If I was to put all my energy into walking, I might be able to take a few steps, but only for the sake of it. I'm going to be a wheelchair-user when I get out of here.'

This didn't make sense. Jen and Steph and even my

mum told me it was right to hope. Hope was what had got me through the past three weeks. How could Simon be so negative? But now I was here in the hospital and saw the sheer awfulness of what Simon was going through, I realised I'd been deluding myself. I'd been a fool. I felt stupid and scared and desperate to get out. I mumbled something about letting Dan have a turn and backed away. I wasn't really aware of what they chatted about after that. I was just trying to control myself. It was all much worse than I'd imagined.

That was when Sylvia came in. 'Time's up for now, you two,' she said. 'The nurses need to come in for a moment.'

I was so glad. Then I thought: I must say goodbye properly, so I approached Si again, to kiss him. I wanted to kiss him – but for his sake, not for mine. So I leant over him and my lips made contact with his cheek. I was careful to avoid the drip and its milky liquid. It was like kissing an old person. There seemed to be no response from him. I backed out, muttering about coming again soon and, once I was outside, I thought: where can I go and cry? I looked around. I didn't want to break down in front of Simon's mum and Danny's parents. I looked wildly around me. Then someone took my arm – one of the nurses – and said, 'Are you Simon's girlfriend?'

I nodded. She guided me down the corridor and into a little room. She shut the door, and a wail broke from me – a wail like a wounded animal, a cry that contained everything: my shock and horror, my pity for Simon, my self-pity, my knowledge that my world and his world would never be the same again.

The nurse put her arm around me. 'It's okay,' she said. 'Let it all out.'

DANNY

A nurse saw Emma was going to lose it completely and she took her off somewhere. That was a relief. I didn't know what to say to her. How could I reassure Emma when I was fighting to keep cool myself?

My parents came over and said was I okay? Me? That was a laugh. Even though I was out of the ward now, my mind was still fixed on Simon, Simon lying on his bed like an old man, head back, on a drip. I wondered what the nurses were doing to him now. I could feel something rising in my chest, a surge of molten anguish, and I breathed hard to push it back down. There was no point in giving vent to my feelings, no point at all.

I took some more deep breaths and I felt my parents watching me, my mum's eagle glance taking in how I was feeling, careful not to come over and intervene. My parents have always respected my personal space. There have been times when I wished they were a bit more comfortable with things. Now I was glad they were leaving me alone. I put a hand on the wall to steady myself.

So. It was every bit as bad as I had thought. And if I hadn't cancelled on him, this never would have happened.

I was in this as deeply as Simon. I was going back in there in a moment and I was going to make damn sure he knew that I was going to be there for him all the time, constantly, unwaveringly. He may have lost the use of his legs, but he hadn't lost me. I was in this for the long haul and, however difficult it was going to be, well, it was less than I deserved.

The nurses came out smiling and laughing, which was bizarre. How could you work in a place like this and be happy? I walked purposefully back to Simon but this time I was prepared, no staring around me and cracking inane jokes.

I stood over him. Our eyes locked.

'I'm sorry,' I said.

'So am I.' He attempted a smile.

'No, I mean about cancelling on you, so that you played in the match.'

Simon looked puzzled for an instant, then his face cleared.

'Dan,' he said. 'If you hadn't cancelled, I'd have rung you and cancelled myself. I wanted to play in the match. It was my choice.'

I wanted to say, do you really mean that? But it would have sounded lame. And my throat was tight with emotion – I couldn't speak, even if I'd planned to.

'This is nobody's fault,' Simon said. 'Not even the guy I collided with. I was watching the ball, Dan, only the ball. I didn't see him going for it too.'

'So you don't blame *him?*' I asked.

Simon's eyes flicked from mine to the ceiling again.

'No. No point. He didn't mean to do it. He was just going for the ball too and he didn't see me. He wrote me a letter and me and Mum answered it. It was just a freak accident, like being hit by lightning or something. But it's happened, so I've got to cope with it.'

Those were the bravest words I had ever heard in my life. Then I realised this: always, all my life, I'd looked up to Simon. I knew he was better than me in every way – cleverer, fitter, better-looking – and it always killed me that we were such good mates. What confidence I had came from being Simon's chosen friend. Now here he was lying useless on a bed – and he was likely to be there for a very long time. But I still looked up to him. Not just because he was being brave, but because there was something about him that hadn't changed. He was still Simon, still completely himself, and the fact his body wasn't working and his legs were screwed and there were weights holding his head down meant nothing. They didn't change the relationship between us at all, not one bit.

Could I say any of this to him? Are you joking? But I stood there by him and he knew.

'What can I do?' I asked Simon.

'Visit,' he said. 'I like you being here.'

'Sorted,' I said.

'Get me some decent music to listen to?'

'Done,' I said, and we discussed albums. Then school, and people's reactions. But not Emma, he never mentioned her once.

But he did say, 'So what about Mr Neale? Are you still under threat of being kicked out?'

'Nah,' I said. 'That's all sorted. Everything's fine.'

Simon just stared at the ceiling and I couldn't tell whether he believed my lie or not. Anyway, whatever. I *really* didn't give a toss now about school. All that mattered was being there for Simon. End of story.

I asked Simon about the unit and he said the nurses were cool, really friendly and good at making sure you weren't embarrassed. Then I saw his eyes closing and realised he was tired.

'You want to rest?' I asked.

'Yeah.'

' 'Kay. I'll be back tomorrow,' I told him. 'See you then,' and I came out.

I grinned at my parents. 'I'm fine,' I reassured them.

EMMA

It was frightening, the way I couldn't stop myself crying. And embarrassing too. The nurse stayed with me, passing me tissues, waiting. Once I calmed down and the sobs stopped ripping me apart, she asked, 'What's your name?'

I told her. She said, 'I'm Tracey.'

I tried to smile at her. It seemed wrong, smiling.

'How long have you two been going out, then?'

'Almost six months.'

'So it's serious?'

I nodded. I was definitely calming down now. Though the realisation that I was glad to be out of Simon's ward filled me with guilt.

'He's nice, your boyfriend,' Tracey said.

I looked up at her, gratefully. She was blonde, a pretty, full face, and she wore glasses with a blue frame. I thought she was probably five or six years older than me.

'I'll be all right,' I said. 'You can go and nurse some patients,' I said. I didn't want to be wasting her time.

'No, Emma. Part of what we do is help families and partners. This is the first time you've visited, isn't it?'

I nodded.

'I thought I hadn't seen you until today.' We exchanged friendly smiles again. 'This is the worst it'll be,' Tracey said. 'Next time you see him, you'll be prepared. It'll get better.'

I knew that. There was something else I wanted to ask her. Quite simply: 'Will he walk again?'

She shook her head.

'But with all the new research?'

'No.' Her voice was sombre. Then she took my hand. 'Emma, you're not going to like what I'm going to say, but someone's got to do this. It might be better if you finish with Simon now. Six months isn't that long and both of you are very young. You're not going to be able to have a proper relationship, not now – and even when he's finished rehab, he won't be . . . He won't have any real control in all of the lower part of his body. Even some wives find they can't cope. If you feel you need to finish with him, no one will blame you. If I was to sit here and tell you it's going to be easy, or even possible, to have a normal relationship, I'd be lying.' A long silence, unbroken by either of us. Then she said, 'You hate me, don't you?'

'No,' I said. 'I'm glad you've said all that.'

And I was. Because now I knew what it was I wanted to do.

SIMON

It's dark now and I don't know what the time is. The nurses think I'm sleeping. But just a moment ago my mind snapped awake and I replayed the afternoon and Danny and Emma's visit. Up till now, this whole mess has been an ordeal, but an ordeal I'm handling okay. I've put up with pain, with discomfort, with humiliation. I'm learning to take one day at a time.

Then Dan and Emma walked in and for the first time I realised what I'd lost. And that was the worst moment so far, worse even than when the doctor told me how bad my injury was. I could see on their faces what I'd become.

A tear falls from me and I try to move my hand to wipe it away, but my fingers are still refusing to obey my commands and they just knock uselessly against the side of my face. Another tear. I think of Dan and how it feels like he's my link to the world. And I think of Emma.

I remember the horror on her face when she saw me and the way Dan had to put her hand on mine. She is so beautiful, and I felt bad for being the reason she had to come to this place. I'm telling myself now the thing I couldn't admit before. It's over. Our relationship is over. I've not just lost the use of my body, but I've lost her too. There are more tears. I'm crying properly now and I'm surprised. I never cry – and even since the accident, I hadn't cried once. When my mum wept, I didn't. Now my face is wet and I feel myself convulsing with sobs that seem to be coming from somewhere else, not from me.

Emma. Emma, Emma. She's so out of reach now and I can't bear the thought. I want her. But it's over. I'm alone, completely alone, and scared, and I want to wake up and find this is all a nightmare.

But this is my reality now.

EMMA

Danny was sitting at the back of the pub and he had already bought himself a pint. As I threaded my way through the crowd towards him he looked up, saw me, and smiled. He insisted on getting me something, but I didn't want anything alcoholic – I told him an orange juice would do.

They're not too fussy about checking out your age at the Coach and Horses, which is why we often used to go there. Anyway, Danny could easily pass for eighteen or older. He's built on a big scale. I watched him, his back to me, hoping to get the barman's attention. I felt very calm, in the way you do when you've made your mind up. Over a week had elapsed since I first saw Simon in the hospital and since then we'd both been back a few times to see him. Each time it had become a little easier, in that there was no shock, but also a little harder, as we began to realise that Simon's life had changed for ever. As had all of our lives.

I decided I wanted to speak to Danny first, even before my mother. Mum had asked me what I wanted to do about Simon and, like Tracey, she said no one would blame me if we finished our relationship. I said I knew that. Neither Jen nor Steph had asked me about what I was going to do. They would have thought it was cheeky. I just knew they would be on my side whatever I did. I could have chosen them to speak to first, but I didn't feel they could take in the whole situation, because they hadn't *seen* Simon yet. Danny alone was the person who could understand my predicament. It was him I wanted to talk to. I'd suggested we meet in the pub, and so here we were, and Danny was carrying over my orange juice. He was wearing a drab olive hoodie and jeans. He came and sat next to me.

'Dan,' I said. 'Why do you never wear the shirt Si bought you for your birthday?'

He shrugged. 'I dunno. It seems like a kind of mockery.'

'I guess. Like that was a happy shirt, and you don't feel good now?'

He nodded. 'Too right.'

I smiled. We talked about Simon's progress for a bit. There was no change. He was still in halo traction and he seemed to me to be losing weight. He'd told us that was inevitable. Dan had joked he ought to try it as he could do with dropping a stone or two. You'd think that was tactless, but Simon smiled. I'll never understand men and their black humour. It felt right, sitting there with Danny. We'd been through a lot together in the last few weeks. So it was quite easy and natural to bring up the subject I'd intended.

'Do you remember the first time we saw Simon and that nurse had to take me away?'

'Yeah. You never told me what she'd said to you. We were all in a bit of a mess.'

'Basically, she gave it to me straight. She said I'd be better off breaking with Simon now. She told me I shouldn't hope to ever have a proper relationship with him again.'

Danny put his drink down and looked at me. That helped. I'm the kind of person who gains strength from other people's reactions. They point me in the direction I need to go in. I watch people's faces carefully. Now, Danny was apprehensive, unsure, and I knew what he was thinking. How could I drop Simon just because of what had happened? He was Simon's best mate. He saw things from Simon's point of view. So I said: 'How can I finish with Simon now, when he needs me most?'

'Yeah,' Dan said. I sensed his approval and carried on.

'When Tracey – the nurse – spoke to me, it clarified everything. To finish with Simon would have been so selfish and cruel. Anyway . . .' I paused. 'I love him.'

Danny beamed at me. He leant over, put an arm round my shoulders and squeezed me. I felt tears spring to my eyes.

'It's good to hear you say that, Em. I've been worried. I know you've been finding it very hard.'

'It's true, I have. I can't pretend. But I've been thinking and thinking, and Simon's lost so much, and the one thing I can do for him is to make sure he doesn't lose me. I want to be by his side, Dan. I know I can do it. And that's what I've decided.'

'Emma,' Danny said, 'you're a great girl.' He looked at me and smiled. I could see his admiration and pleasure, and I felt deeply grateful and surer than ever that I'd said the right thing. In my own mind, I was relieved too. Because, if I'm being perfectly honest, I worried whether the fact I'd not told anyone my decision for a week was a sign I wasn't sure in my own mind. Or was I just being mature, thinking about things, as my mum said adults do? No matter. The fact was, I'd committed myself. I'd made my vow.

'Em,' Dan continued. 'If I can help you at all, whatever you want me to do – just say. I'm with you on this one.'

I nodded, my heart full. We were silent for a moment or two. Then I carried on.

'I'm not going to say this to Simon – there's no need. Why should he ever question that I wouldn't be there for him? I'll only tell him if he brings up the subject of our relationship.'

'Good thinking.'

I loved having Danny's approval and it made the whole thing easier for me. I felt calm and pure and happy – no, not happy. I would never be completely happy again. But I felt I'd been true to my feelings to Simon before the accident and I could live with myself now. I was under no illusions. I knew I would have to learn to love him all over again, in a way. I didn't mind the feeling of testing myself.

Danny finished his pint. I wanted to give him money for

the next round but he absolutely refused. He said he still had all his birthday money – he'd never got round to spending it and didn't want to. I could understand that. This time I said I'd have some vodka with my orange. I felt as if I needed a drink, even as if I *deserved* one. Because the point about true love – it has to overcome adversity. Think of Romeo and Juliet, and—

A text came through on my phone. It was Jen, asking me what I was doing. I texted back that I was in the Coach and Horses with Dan. She said she and Steph were bored – could they join us? I said yes. She said she'd be there in a moment as they were just round the corner at Steph's place. I had this feeling that my friends were rallying round – and it was good.

When Dan came back with the drinks, he smiled at me as he put them carefully on the table. He said: 'I've been bothered about you, Em. It was cool you told me how you were feeling. It's the same for me. I can't talk to my mum and dad because . . . it's hard to say. Like, in our family, you have to just get on with things. Which is right, yeah? But I just want to tell someone how angry I feel, that this could happen. Sometimes I just put the music on loud in my room and just shout and swear and stuff. But I'm still . . . like . . . I keep thinking it should have been me – and I didn't realise life was so unfair. I make myself imagine what Simon's going through. And then at school, I've still got Mr Neale hassling me, and Simon asked—'

'Emma! Danny!' Jen squealed as she dodged through the drinkers. Steph was in her wake.

I glanced at Danny. He had frozen in mid-speech. If only they'd arrived a moment or two later, when he'd finished speaking. Or that I'd have a chance to warn him they were coming. But in a flash he was the old Danny, jumping to his feet, teasing them, planting a big kiss on Jen's lips, fooling around in full-on Danny mode. It was strange, the way he switched moods so quickly. Just click and . . .

DANNY

'You two just can't keep away, can you? Come here, Jen! That's better. What can I get you?'

I didn't want Jen and Steph in on my talk with Emma. That was private stuff, meant only for her ears. And if I didn't get another chance, well, whatever. Jen insisted on buying the next round and she pushed her way over to the bar. Steph had taken my seat next to Emma, so I sat opposite. Steph told me they'd texted Adam and Wilko to invite them and they were on their way. I grinned, said it was cool. But I thought: this is the first time we'd all been together since my birthday. I took a long gulp of beer. Smelt cigarette smoke, beer fumes; saw faces and bodies; heard some cheesy boy-band anthem on the sound system. Thought: I'm out for the night, I'm supposed to be enjoying myself. Let's see if it's possible.

So when Jen got back I pulled her onto my lap, took a swig of her vodka and orange, and washed it down with my beer. Wilko and Adam came in from the back door – I guessed they'd come in Adam's car. He'd turned seventeen at the beginning of September, took one of those intensive courses in driving, passed his test, and his parents – who are loaded – bought him his wheels. Wilko clocked what I was drinking and made his way to the bar. Adam took a seat on the other side of Emma. His designer cologne wafted over to me. I drank some more beer.

Someone turned the music up, so we had to shout. Wilko and I talked football – our team was playing badly. Adam butted in – said it was pathetic, as season ticket holders he and his dad had a right to expect some improvement. Jen wriggled off my lap and sat by Steph. Footie-talk bored her.

And there we all were, our group, our clique, closing in, making a unit – except it felt to me as if we were malformed. No Simon. I never realised before how much he was the centre of things – we all looked to him for approval. He didn't talk as much as me, he wasn't as cool as Adam, and he certainly didn't drink as much as Wilko. But we depended on him. Only what was bugging me was that I was the only one who seemed to be recognising it. Everyone else was behaving just as they always did. Wilko attempted to down his pint in one. I challenged him.

Quick trip for a pee. Back again, pub busier, noisier, steady bass from the sound system. Yeah, I'm feeling good, kind of. Bit clumsy, apologise to a bloke whose pint I unsettle as I brush against him. Back to our table, everyone listening to Adam.

'My dad's going to try his best. Simon's parents are going to see him tomorrow. Injuries aren't his main field but he's going to personally oversee this.'

Emma directed a huge smile at him.

'What was all that about?' I asked.

Adam explained. His dad's a solicitor and he was going to look into suing the school for negligence, on Simon's behalf.

'But it wasn't anybody's fault,' I said.

Adam shook his head. 'Simon should have been rested. The coach shouldn't have asked him to play. He should have been warned against the kind of manoeuvre that ended in his accident.'

I frowned. Maybe the beer was befuddling me. I didn't get it.

'But Simon wanted—'

Adam interrupted. 'Dan, don't you remember how Neale told us first thing on that Monday morning that it was no one's fault? That was to get the school off the hook.'

Emma reached over and took my hand. 'Danny,' she said meaningfully. 'Simon needs the money. Adam was explaining. If they sue successfully, it could make a huge difference. Simon can get special equipment, trips abroad, maybe for advanced treatment – it's worth doing. And Adam's dad isn't charging. And Adam also says that the school is insured for this sort of thing. It won't be the school that pays out, but just some insurance firm. It is *so* worth doing!'

Okay. Think of me as vermin if you like, but I wasn't happy. It was something to do with the way Adam was smirking and almost capitalising on the situation to turn himself into Mr Big. And there was Emma, believing again everything was going to be fine and smiling up at Adam, who was now whispering something to her that made her laugh. What? Was it about me? How could she smile and laugh when I still felt like . . . I drank some more beer.

'Nice one, Dan,' Wilko said. 'Next round on me.'

Which was Wilko's way of trying to say he knew what I'd been going through. I appreciated that. I tried to punch him in the arm and missed. Slipped a bit, but righted myself.

'You okay?' Jen said.

'No, come here,' I commanded. I lunged at her and she struggled, but not that much. I tried one of those sloppy romantic kisses and pushed her back. She was trying to wriggle away and Steph called out to stop it otherwise we'd get thrown out. So I did. Emma shot me an odd look. I thought, the drink isn't working. I still wasn't happy. There was a dull ache inside me that wouldn't go away

Distorted waves of chatter and music and a cry of, 'Last orders!' I'm shattered, feeling slightly sick. Stumble off to the Gents again, come back, sit next to Steph. Time to explain.

'I'm not feeling good,' I said.

'Just take it easy,' she said, concerned. Steph is pretty: long curly hair, wide eyes, the kind of girl who always has a listening face on. Jen is more of the babe: dead-straight blonde hair, low-cut tops that draw your eyes down her cleavage. But now I felt like talking to Steph.

'I'm not feeling goo',' I said again, to make my point.

'Do you want to go back to the Gents?'

'Not feeling goo' about Simon,' I explained.

I looked over at Emma. She was talking intently to Adam. What was she telling him? Why wasn't she telling me?

'It won't be long before you and Simon can get drunk together,' Steph said. 'But do you think we ought to go? Are you going to be okay for school tomorrow?'

'School can sod off. I'm leaving anyway.'

'Danny!'

'Or they're kicking me out. I'm tired.' I rested my head on her shoulder. Adam got to his feet.

'I'll give Dan a lift back but I want one of you in the back with him in case he throws up.'

'That'll be me,' said Emma.

I was frogmarched out to the car park. The cold air was making me queasy. It was funny, the way Adam clicked on his key fob and the car answered him by flashing its lights. It made me laugh; it was like his car was talking to him. Emma didn't know what I was laughing at.

In the back with Emma. Adam keeps the car steady and I don't think I'm going to be sick. So I lean against Emma and she smells great, all soft and warm, and her hair tickles my face. Emma belongs to Simon. Pretend to click on a key fob in front of Emma and say, 'Talk to me.' She doesn't know what I'm on about. Need a pee badly. That's why I don't fall asleep and why I'm not sick.

Home. Helped out of car, tell them I have the key. I think they stay till I work out how to open the front door, but I don't remember. I managed the stairs, though once or twice I felt myself falling, bumping into the banister. Shout to Mum and Dad that I'm home, and lock myself in the bathroom.

There for ages. Waves of nausea surge through me. A beer-sodden, stinking wreck, that's what I am. Stupid, disgusting, vile. But now I just wanna go to bed.

And I lie there, still dressed, legless. Can't move. A blanket of oblivion suffocates me and stops all thought, all movement.

SIMON

I think it must be well on into the morning from the noises outside. Have I slept longer than usual? I'm groggy, drugged and my mouth is sticky. There's my ceiling above me. There's a strange tingling in my legs, like they want to wake up and can't.

Nothing has changed, everything is the same. I hear the nurses moving about outside. I try to remember what I was dreaming. I wait for a nurse to come and move me and see to the drips. And after a space of time Tracey arrives and chats and does what she has to do. I'm grateful for the company. She tells me the latest gossip. She says they've moved someone else into the ward but I don't really listen. I'm wondering whether the tingling in my legs is a sign I'm getting feeling back, and I ask her. 'No,' she said, 'everyone gets that.' And she goes.

Everyone tells me I'll never walk again and it's hard to give up hope. But I can see what they mean – dreaming of a miracle stops you dealing with the here and now. So that's why I've made my world shrink to this ward and this bed and I'm beginning to feel as if I don't need what I had before. The glimpse of a person walking by is an event. I look forward to the nurses coming and to my visitors. Though sometimes it's painful, being forced to re-enter the outside world.

Last night Mum was hyper. She was telling me how good they've been at work. Her boss is letting her reduce her hours so she can be here more often. She said she'd like to learn about the passive exercise I'm doing, so she can help. I don't know how I feel about that. I don't mind the nurses coming over and moving my legs and arms so the muscles don't waste. But my mum? She told me all about Adam's dad and the idea of suing the school. I couldn't see that working. She explained how we could use the money. She would get an extension built so when I came home I could have a room and bathroom leading off from the lounge at the back of the house. She wanted to get the kitchen altered – someone had told her that I would need everything to be at a lower level if I was to be able to make some toast or get a drink. Planning like that, I reckoned, helped her cope.

I asked her where Dad was. 'Looking after David?' I asked. But instantly I regretted my question. That bitter, resigned look took up residence in her face, the one that made me automatically ask her what was wrong, even though I didn't want to.

'He's finding this hard, Simon,' she said, levelly, neutrally.

'I know.'

'He's working late tonight. That's why he says he can't be with us.'

I said nothing. I knew what my mum was thinking. I've always had this ability, since I was a kid. It's not the same as being close to your mum. It's more that there's a window in my head that lets me see into her head. When there was all the trouble a few years ago with Dad, I was the only person who knew what was going on and knew what to do to help her. Mum said – and I knew she was going to say this – 'He's withdrawing from the situation. It's the only way he can handle it. He leaves the decisions to me. His trouble is that . . .'

He can't face up to things, I finished silently for her. I suppose that's why I *can* face up to things. There's always been this idea that I would not be like my father – except I am, in some ways. He likes everything to be easy and happy and perfect. So do I. I can understand why he finds this big change hard. I also understand why my mum despises him for that. I can see all these things very clearly but I can't do anything about them. My mum has it hard, I know. And now she has it harder than ever.

When she went, I was pleased. I turned my mind away from her, telling myself that my parents would have to deal with their own problems. A nurse came and I asked her to fix up the headphones and the cassette player so I could listen to Danny's music. I asked her to turn it up as loud as possible.

Now, this morning, I think I was selfish last night. My mum needed sympathy and I didn't give her any. I hoped she wasn't going to lean too much on David, in my absence. I'm quite protective towards my younger bro, and it was funny, the few times he had been to visit me, I felt awkward, as if I didn't want him to see me like this, as if I was letting him down. With Dan, of course, it's different. He is the one person I feel normal with.

Still no nurses. I decide to replay an old rugby match in my head to pass the time. Then I wonder how much movement I'll get back in my fingers. Will I be able to write again? Or will my handwriting change? I know it's wrong to worry, so now I try to remember films I've seen. I decide to go over—

'Hello!'

Someone's shouting at me. Who? Where?

'What's your name?'

'Simon,' I say, unsure where the voice is coming from. A male voice, local accent.

'I'm Pete. What happened to you?'

I realise now. It's the person in the next bed. I feel myself getting self conscious and nervous.

'I collided with a guy in a rugby match. I've broken my C7 and dislocated my C6. I'm in halo traction.'

'Bummer. I've just come out of mine. I'm a complete C7 and I fractured my skull. I swerved to avoid a cat, didn't I? And hit a lamppost. The wife, she comes out of it with just bruising and shock. And I break my bloody back.'

But his tone is amused, deprecating. I ask, 'And the car?'

'Not a car. A motorbike. A Harley. Complete and utter write-off.'

'Shame.'

'Yeah, but you know, here's a thing. I'm lying there, I know it's serious, I'm still conscious and waiting for the ambulance and I have this feeling I'm never going to walk again. But I'm resigned. It was like I always knew it was going to happen. Did you get that?'

'No, not at all.'

'Do you remember what happened to you?'

'No,' I say truthfully. 'I remember nothing. I remember seeing the ball – and the next thing, I'm waking up here and there's a doctor standing over me.'

'Were you in IC?'

'In Intensive Care? No – they told me I just had a few days in the hospital being stabilised, then I was transferred here.'

'You were lucky. I had all sorts go wrong. Two weeks in IC, then I had to wait for a bed here. But it was worth it. This place is the DBs.'

'The DBs?'

He coughs, embarrassed. 'The dog's bollocks, mate.'

'How was it,' I ask, 'coming out of traction?'

'There was this *click* – that was my head snapping back into place – then I feel my head lift itself off the pillow like I'm levitating. But that's normal, I'm told. Now I can move it around a bit. Still not got much of an appetite, though. You on a drip still?'

'Yeah,' I said.

'Tough. How old are you, Simon?'

'Sixteen.'

Now there was a pause. I could tell he was taken aback, possibly feeling sorry for me. I didn't want that, so I filled in the gap as quickly as I could. 'And you?'

'Thirty-four.'

'And you're married?'

'For three years. Two kiddies as well, Kyle and Britney. They're four and two.'

I thought about how it would be for them, having a dad in a wheelchair. Pete seemed to read my mind.

'Every day when I wake up, I think how lucky I am. Because my kids have still got their dad. They'll be coming in later, making a racket. It's tough on the wife, I know. It's her I worry about. But we're all together, right? I'm here, aren't I? In the land of the living?'

I hear that cliché and weigh it up. I don't think of the unit as a place of the living, but as a shadow land, where minds are trapped in broken bodies. But I was wrong and Pete was right. This is the land of the living.

'So what about you, Simon? You got a girlfriend?'

I hesitate. This is the first time I've spoken about Emma to anyone. She belongs to the past. I still didn't know whether she would be part of my future.

'Yes. I did before my accident. Emma.'

'Seen her since?'

'Yeah, she visits.'

More silence. I broke in. 'With Danny, my best mate. There's also my mum and dad and my little brother, David. And various other family members.'

'You feel like a freak show at times, don't you?'

'Yeah,' I said.

Another silence. This is the oddest conversation I've ever had. I'm lying on my bed staring at the ceiling and this voice is coming at me. Almost like you'd imagine God to speak to you. Except this voice has a strong local accent. But not seeing someone, you're not forced to take their reactions into account. You can say exactly what's on your mind.

'Do you imagine yourself walking again?' I ask.

'They tell you not to, and they're right. But you can't give up on hope, can you? That's why we buy a lottery ticket every week, me and the wife.'

That was the conclusion I'd reached and I felt heartened. I know that really I'm not going to walk again, but I like to dream I might. There were more sounds outside and I reckoned a meal was on its way to those who could eat. Someone laughed, out by the nurses' station.

'Morning,' says Becky, coming into our ward with a trolley. We both greet her. 'You two been getting to know each other, then?' We agree. Becky's a big girl, she reminds me of Dawn French. She takes Pete his breakfast and I find

I'm smiling. I'm imagining his pleasure at getting some real food to eat.

Later on, Pete talks some more. He tells me about his mates and their bike club. He's a gas fitter. His dad used to be a miner until they closed the pits. His uncle as well – and he had also broken his back. Pete said, even in a wheelchair he could down a pint as well as the next man. I listen to all of this and imagine myself in Pete's world.

When his wife arrives later, Pete introduces me and she comes over to say hello. Her name is Sheila. She has dyed blonde hair with the roots showing, a bright pink sweater, a denim skirt. She goes back to Pete and jokes that I'm much better-looking than he is.

'You leave my wife alone,' he shouts over.

'I'm making no promises,' I call back, and smile again.

I'm tired, and I drift off. But now, when I wake, there's someone there, someone who's going through what I am. I tell Pete about Mum and Dad trying to sue the school and how I don't like the idea. 'It was only my fault,' I said. 'No one else's.'

Pete disagrees. 'You could do with the money,' he tells me. 'When you get out of here, you'll want to be independent, a lad like you. You'll need an adapted car, special equipment – listen, the more dosh you have, the better. Your school'll be insured anyway. They can afford it more than you.'

I consider that. But I can't imagine ever getting out of

here, and a part of me doesn't want to. I want this thing off my head, and I want to get into physio, but I'm safe in here.

Pete asks me how my family have taken it. I immediately feel myself clamming up, but decide that – who knows? – I might tell him a little more another day. 'They've been brilliant,' I say. Then I change the subject and tell him about Danny, how he's been coming most every night.

'A good mate,' Pete says. 'You'll need him.'

I agree, but then I find myself saying, 'I reckon he's finding it harder than me, in some ways.' I've noticed a tension in Dan, something simmering away. It's hard to put that into words, so I don't.

'Yeah,' Pete says. 'It's easy, lying here, to think you're the centre of the universe, but the people around us are affected too. My mate Jason has sold his bike, just as a result of me.'

'Will you miss your Harley?' I ask him.

'Me? Nah? I'm gonna get a motorised wheelchair, 500cc. You won't see me for the dust.' He laughs to himself. I smile.

'I won't be able to play rugby again,' I say, and I'm surprised to find a tremble in my voice.

'Bollocks,' Pete says. 'You can play rugby in a wheelchair. You should speak to Tiny Tim.'

'Tiny Tim?'

'Haven't you met him yet? He's a support worker. Big bloke, throws the discus. Got his injury twelve years ago. Complete T2. He'll be round soon enough.'

We talk some more, until I get tired. Time has never

passed more quickly. When we break off, for the first time since my accident I feel completely alive. I realise this is because I've been speaking to someone as an equal. I haven't been peered down at by the able-bodied or the staff, but someone's taken my injury for granted and talked to me. I wasn't alone any more.

Tiny Tim? Wheelchair rugby? What was all that about? You can't play rugby in a wheelchair, whatever Pete says. What does he know? But obviously there *is* something called wheelchair rugby – and it might be like rugby. Half of me can't be bothered to find out, but the rest of me is curious. And I think that maybe, one day, I might try to check it out. Or maybe not. But you could be pretty fast in a wheelchair, if you really went for it . . .

EMMA

I visited Simon last night. It was a good visit. Mum was able to take me as she had the evening off. The tree by the nurses' station was loaded with baubles and tinsel, and there were presents scattered nearby it. There were decorations everywherc. Simon's bed was festooned with them. When I got in I bent over and kissed him. I'm quite proud of myself now, as the drip and halo don't bother me at all. I asked Simon how he was and he said he'd had a good day. He told me about Pete in the next bed and how his physio was going. I could tell Simon was dying to get to that stage, but the good news is the doctors are saying that his Christmas present might be the removal of the halo traction. I like getting involved in the details of Simon's treatment. I sat by the bed and we talked and I was glad, glad I was there for him, doing the right thing. Last night it didn't bother me that we'd never talked about our relationship. Sometimes I wanted to, but I was waiting for Simon to bring the subject up. Last night it felt right just to take everything for granted, just to leave things as they were. It was comforting to assume that everything was the same as ever.

Going back in the car, I thought: do I still love him? The

reply came – of course I do, but it's a different kind of love now. It was my turn to do the loving, as he couldn't at the moment. And maybe I would always have to be the one who gives. Which was okay, I thought, I could do that. There's a loveliness about Simon that's still there, even though he's a thin, feeble shadow of himself. He's skinny now, always dressed in trackies. His hands are kind of curled, his fingers don't work properly. But as I told my mum, it's like an illness, and he will get better. Once he's out of traction and doing physio, he'll be able to sit up for short spells, and then they'll get him in a wheelchair, and then . . .

People are nice to me. I don't know what I would have done without my friends. Just as I have to be there for Simon, Jen and Steph have been there for me. I know I can ring Steph any time and she'll listen and console me. Jen is always on at me to make sure I enjoy myself too. She says I need a life and I see what she means, but I'm quite happy just visiting Simon. That's my role.

Yes, everyone seems to appreciate how hard it is and that kind of makes things easier. The boys too. Dan's still down, of course, but that's partly because Mr Neale won't let up on him. We all think he's being a bit tight, especially as it's Christmas.

I thought all those things as I walked into school on the last day of term. The day we break up for Christmas is usually the best day in the school calendar. The Sixth Form dress up and deliver the charity Christmas cards. None of the teachers make us do any work, and there's the carol service in the afternoon. There's a party atmosphere everywhere.

So there I was, both looking forward to the day and conscious all the time of Simon – I'll tell you what it's like, like a tune you can't get out of your head. I was going about my daily routine and the tune of Simon – sad, slow, broken – is playing all the time, sometimes swelling loud, and at other times dying away almost into silence, then rushing back into a full crescendo.

But just then it was hardly audible. School was fizzing with excitement. Every classroom had decorations up, kids were opening presents, and some Year Nine girls passed me with tinsel in their hair. When I arrived in the Sixth Form centre everyone was gathered in the middle of the room. I soon saw what had happened. Some people had rigged up our tree to the ceiling so it was suspended a foot off the ground. I went over to my locker. The paper-chains that we'd put up at the beginning of the week were partly falling down. But the mistletoe was still intact, hanging over the door that led out to the chocolate machine. The radio was full blast, playing Christmas songs.

Jen came over to say all the girls were wearing bunches today. She got hold of my hair and divided it into two, then tied it with tinsel high up, so I looked like a proper old-fashioned schoolgirl. She completed the ensemble with some freckles on my cheek that she drew on with her eyebrow pencil. I didn't dare look in the mirror.

Then Adam came in. We'd got quite friendly lately as he was keeping me posted about Simon's claim against the school. Yesterday night his dad had dinner with a friend who specialises in medical claims. Adam also wanted to do Law. He reckoned with eight GCSEs at A* and one at A, he stood a good chance of Oxbridge.

He saw me immediately and came over.

'Hi, Emma.'

There was something a little flat in his voice. I frowned at him.

'Not good news, I'm afraid.'

We sat down on some chairs near my locker. He took his parka off and put it on the chair back.

'You know that meeting yesterday, between my dad and his friend from London? It doesn't look good.'

'Why?' I asked. The Simon tune was playing loudly now.

'He doesn't feel Simon has a case. He couldn't see any sign of negligence on the part of the school. He doesn't think it's worth taking forward. He said it might cause more hassle for everyone concerned. He thought it was better to take the charity route – contact rugby federations, things like that.'

'Oh.' I tried to digest the news. I'd allowed myself to hope that there would be money. I knew Simon's family needed it. His mum had converted her job to part-time so she could visit him more and, when he came home, they'd have to adjust the house, possibly make an extension and build him his own room, not to mention the equipment he'd need. This was bad. Adam said we'd have to contact some charities. Or maybe we could do some fundraising, only we'd need thousands and thousands. I felt so powerless – I didn't know what to say.

Adam took my hand. 'I'm pretty gutted too,' he said. He stroked my fingers. 'But we mustn't give up. Dad's going to get in touch with as many of his contacts as possible. We'll find a way.' He squeezed my hand and let it go. I felt very close to him just then. I appreciated the way he was trying to do something practical for Simon. 'I bet you don't feel much like Christmas, Em,' he said.

'No,' I replied. That wasn't entirely true. An opposite feeling washed over me – I *wanted* it to be Christmas; I wanted to have permission to enjoy myself; I wanted an end to all of this misery, for me, for Simon, for everyone.

Then Adam said: 'I think you look great in pigtails.' He winked at me. And I thought: he knows how I'm feeling. He sensed my mood. So I smiled back at him and there was a pact between us – I knew it – that just for a short time, we would have fun. Like Jen said, I needed a life. And when better than Christmas?

'Hey,' he said. 'I've got something for you.'

From his bag he brought out a carefully wrapped present. It had my name on it. I unwrapped it to discover an Armani perfume gift set – it must have cost loads!

'Are you sure?' I said, which was a bit pathetic, but I was lost for words.

'You deserve it,' he said. 'More than anyone I know.'

I hugged him tight and – because I'm telling the truth – it felt good to hug him. A boy hug is different from a girl hug. It's exciting – you always feel there could be more to it. And it flashed into my mind that I was missing that sense of being found attractive. To everyone I'd become a tragedy queen, a nun, the untouchable girlfriend-widow of Simon. It was true – I *was* that person – but I was also Emma and only sixteen, a normal girl, and there was no reason why I couldn't be me and be there for Simon too. So I hugged Adam back and kissed him on his cheek. When we broke away, I could see he was blushing. And I felt good – no, more than good – a bit giddy, breathless, slightly wild and ready to roll.

Steph arrived next and once she'd taken off her coat she attached a pair of golden wings to her back, tied some tinsel round her head like a headband, and was the perfect Christmas angel. We all gathered round and she distributed her presents to us. Jen was exclaiming over a gorgeous little necklace Steph had bought her when Dan arrived. He stood by us and I saw him look at me. He wasn't smiling.

'Any news about the meeting yesterday?' he asked. He was also waiting to see what Adam's dad's verdict would be. We all shut up for a moment. I wished Danny would cheer up. Then I hated myself for feeling that, and guilt swept over me – being found like this having a good time. But no – it was Dan who needed to learn how to enjoy himself again.

Adam said, 'It doesn't look good. There really isn't a case.'

'I was asking Emma,' Dan said.

DANNY

Quick as a flash, I didn't even know I was going to say that. Adam was my mate, I knew that, but there was something about the way he was muscling in on . . . I didn't know what his motives were. And I was in a filthy mood. I turned on my heel and walked away, to give myself a chance to cool off.

I think it was the contrast between how I was feeling and all the Christmas madness. Even the teachers looked happy. What was wrong with me that I felt so out of it? Simon was what was wrong, but a couple of nights ago when I was up at the unit, even he seemed to be joining in with the Christmas spirit. It was me, my fault that I couldn't be part of it.

Simon was so much more accepting of what's happened than I was. He was telling me the other night about wheelchairs – the really cool ones, apparently, are lightweight and easily collapsible, but they're not entirely funded by the NHS. And this guy, Pete, in the next bed says there's no reason why Si shouldn't learn to drive when he gets out, though it'll cost a few thou to get a car adapted. They talk quite cheerfully about all of this, but can't they see the whole situation stinks? Simon doesn't have that kind of money. The unfairness of it still fills me with rage.

I was thinking these things in fits and starts as I walked the corridors. I passed by the Year Seven classroom that belonged to David, Si's younger brother. I glanced in and there he was, leaping from desk to desk, showing off in front of his mates. I thought: he'll get in trouble for that. I also thought: he doesn't seem bothered about Simon. No one does, except for me. It's like I'm the only person wearing the reality specs. Even Emma – but I couldn't blame Emma. It was tough for her and she was doing well. As long as certain people laid off her.

I walked as far as the sports hall, then I thought I was acting like an idiot. Maybe one reason I was feeling so out of it was because I was keeping myself away from my mates. If I did go back to the Sixth Form centre I might start to cheer up and get into the swing of things. Lessons were delayed that morning to give the teachers a chance to do some form-filling, and we were supposed to be clearing up. So I turned and retraced my steps.

I thought I might see if I could get my dad to drive me up to the unit tonight. Or I might even get a bus up there as soon as school was finished and blag a lift home. I didn't mind it at the unit. The nurses were cool and when I was with Simon, I didn't feel as bad. School was worse, somehow. And I suspected Mr Neale wasn't going to let me go today without another of his little chats.

There were the chocolate machines – I was nearly back in the centre. I prepared myself to face my mates and maybe join in some of the partying. I lifted my head, looked straight in front of me, and there, under the mistletoe, was Emma. There was someone kissing her. Not Simon, though I've never seen anyone kissing Emma but Simon. But hold on – wait a minute – it was Adam kissing Emma. A real kiss, a proper one. Emma's head was tilted back, her eyes were closed; she looked just like she did when Simon kissed her. Only it was Adam she was kissing. He held her tight, as tight as he could. The bastard. And it was like my own blood rose up and blinded me.

'Break it up,' I called out and pulled Adam off her. Emma looked shocked and guilty.

'Chill,' Adam said. 'It's Christmas.'

'Try telling Simon that.' I glared at him, trying to hold back my anger.

'There was nothing in it, Dan, okay? Just lighten up.'

I felt his implied criticism of me and it stung. I wasn't going to let him get away with it. Everyone was watching us. I couldn't back off.

'Emma belongs to Simon,' I said.

'Emma can do what she wants,' Adam replied.

An electric rage pulsed through me.

'You can't kid me,' I said through gritted teeth. 'You've been after her for ages.'

'What's wrong?' Adam asked. 'Are you jealous?'

That was it. Before I knew what had happened, my fist met his jaw. I could hear the crack of knuckle on bone. There was a collective gasp from the crowd. Adam staggered back, blood seeping from his nose. I was shocked but I didn't care. I just wanted to hit him again and again and again. I wanted to pummel him until I couldn't feel my pain any longer.

But as I lunged at him I felt arms constraining me. Some of the lads had got hold of me; I was struggling to fight them off. I don't know what obscenities were coming from my mouth. I was aware that Emma was crying, I think, but that wasn't as important to me as my need to get back at Adam. But someone had taken him away and now, striding through the centre was Mr Neale. And I thought things couldn't get any worse.

The sight of him took the fight out of me. I felt my body sag.

'Daniel – to my office. Now!'

Everyone backed away. I avoided any eye contact as I walked out of the room. I reckoned it was for the last time. There was no way Neale would let me stay on in school after this. I'd become a lout, a thug.

He opened the door of his office and I slunk in. He towered above me, spitting fire.

'There is absolutely *no* excuse for fighting like that, none whatsoever. And you don't have to explain what happened – I saw it all. My patience is up with you. You're going to apologise to Adam and for the rest of the day you can work under supervision, while I contact your parents. And you'll stay in school late tonight to help the cleaners.'

'I can't,' I said. 'I'm going to the unit.'

'You should have thought of that earlier.'

I filled with fury again. 'That's all I am thinking about! That's why I hit him!'

I knew I wasn't making much sense.

'Whatever provocation you had,' Mr Neale continued, rather more measured now, 'there was no excuse for violence.'

I hated the way he sounded right, hated myself, and panicked as I didn't see where this was going to end. I wasn't calming down. I thought: if Adam was to walk in now, I'd still want to hit him.

Mr Neale moved over to his desk and perched on it. I watched him stroke the side of his cheek thoughtfully.

'I know you're feeling angry, but you mustn't take it out on all and sundry.'

I said nothing.

'And you mustn't let what's happened to Simon become an excuse for your own failure to get a grip on your life.'

The unfairness of that cut me to the quick. How dare he go on about my progress at a time like this! Teachers all have one-track minds. I looked up at him, locked eyes and said, 'You don't understand, do you?'

'Don't I?'

It was a strange comment. I thought: does he mean he's also gutted about Simon?

Then he continued. 'You're not the only one who has to cope with tragedy. Five years ago my wife died of cancer. It was before I came here, so you wouldn't know. She was in her thirties. That didn't seem fair to me and there was nothing I could do for her. I also felt angry, angrier than you'll ever know. But it didn't get me anywhere. Besides, I had responsibilities – two very young children. Anger was a luxury I couldn't afford. So, yes, I do understand what you're going through.'

I was staggered. Absolutely staggered. You don't think about your teachers as human beings – and especially as human beings who suffer. The old Mr Neale dissolved in front of my eyes. Now I found a different interpretation for his brusqueness, his temper, his hassled air. And in feeling sorry for him, I stopped feeling sorry for myself.

'Sir,' I said. 'I didn't know.'

He was silent. I looked up at him; his face was set and stern. I began to feel guilty, to hate myself all over again. Then something stirred in me – a realisation that all this self-loathing, all this 'it should have been me' stuff was getting me precisely nowhere. I'd reached a dead end, a cul-de-sac. I was repeatedly ramming my head against a brick wall. Simon was paralysed. That was a fact and beating myself up about it was idiotic and pointless. I had to change my attitude.

Mr Neale said nothing. I said nothing. But it was as if someone had switched on a light. I still wasn't ready to talk about me, though. Instead I questioned Mr Neale.

'Do your kids miss your wife?'

'Not consciously. They were too young to remember her properly.'

'Did she have chemo – or . . .?'

'Yes – we tried everything we could. Conventional medicine, unconventional medicine. But there was a point when we knew were beaten and then we just had to accept. It was easier that way.'

'Like with Si,' I said. 'He has to accept his paralysis. The doctors have told him they're years and years off a realistic method of regenerating the spinal cord.'

Mr Neale nodded. For reasons I didn't fully understand, I found I wanted to talk.

'Did you know Simon's parents are thinking of suing the school? Only to get money. Si's been telling me that it's money that's going to make the biggest difference to him. 'Course you get a wheelchair on the NHS, but if you want a really good one you have to pay extra. And he could learn to drive, if he had an automatic and it was adapted. But Adam is saying they haven't got a case.'

'Is that why you hit him?'

'No! But I could accept Simon's situation better if I thought he had a future. I mean, more of a future than just being an invalid.'

'So why is it,' said Mr Neale – this man has a one-track mind – 'you're not interested in your own future?'

I couldn't answer that, so I moved on. 'If only Simon's family was rich,' I said.

That was when I had the idea. It was as if someone gave it to me, slipped it into my head like a letter coming through the letterbox. I picked up the envelope, opened it, and read the contents.

'*I* could raise some money,' I thought aloud.

'Okay,' said Mr Neale.

'A lot of money. I could get myself sponsored to do something, and set up a fund for Simon, to give him his independence.'

Mr Neale was grinning from ear to ear. 'At last,' he said. 'Danny Harrison is taking action.'

He sounded sarcastic as ever, but his face gave him away. He was delighted and it occurred to me for the first time that Mr Neale actually cared about me and what I was going to do with my life. That it wasn't just a job to him, but something more. That encouraged me. It felt weird to have a teacher on-side, but there you go. Now my mind was in overdrive.

'What could I do?' I asked both him and myself.

Mr Neale said, 'We could certainly arrange a school fundraising event.'

'Okay,' I said, 'but *I* want to do something too. Something to make people sit up and notice.'

'Why don't you run a marathon?'

I thought about that. Me, who got out of breath running for the bus. But it wasn't that which put me off. I wanted to do something that seemed almost impossible. Mind you, running a marathon would have qualified. I am the least fit person I know.

'Everyone runs marathons to raise money,' I said.

'You want to be different.'

'Yeah. I do.'

We were both silent as we thought. Crazy ideas came into my head – sailing round the world, cycling from John O'Groats to Land's End, trekking across the Himalayas. But like Simon, I had to learn to be realistic. I had to do my best, not the impossible.

'Have you got a head for heights?' asked Mr Neale. A bell went. He ignored it.

'Nope. I hate them.'

'So the Three Peaks Challenge is out.'

'What's that?'

'You climb the three mountains of mainland Britain – Ben Nevis, Scafell and Snowdon – in twenty-four hours.'

'You can't do that,' I commented. 'They're too far apart.'

'It can be done,' said Mr Neale. 'You need good transport, a team behind you, but it's possible.'

'Okay,' I told him. 'You're on.'

I don't know why I spoke those words. I just decided there and then that I would go for it. I felt a surge of satisfaction envelop me.

'You mean that?'

'I've never meant anything more in my life.'

'You can count on my support,' Mr Neale said.

'Thank you.'

A totally weird feeling, to realise you've found a new friend and he's a teacher! How was I going to explain this to my mates?

'You'll need to train,' Neale continued. 'And also create as much publicity as possible. We might think of a target and aim to reach that. And you'll have to find a group to go with.'

'No,' I said. 'No. This is something I want to do alone.'

Immediately I knew why. I saw Simon lying on his bed, his head in traction. He would have to make the slow haul back to fitness all by himself. He'd have support, sure, but in the end it was his struggle. I wanted my struggle too. I had to explain.

'I'll do the climbing alone. But I'll have as much help as possible in raising money.'

'I understand,' said Neale, and I knew he did. 'But first you'll go back to the centre and apologise to Adam. You can do the cleaning at lunchtime. I'll trust you to tell your parents what happened today.'

He looked me straight in the eyes. I appreciated the way he was treating me like an adult.

'I will,' I said.

'And in the holidays you're going to make up the work you've missed.'

'Yes.'

I had a lot of catching up to do. Maybe I'd ask Emma for a hand. Her notes were always easy to follow. I'd also tell her about the Three Peaks Challenge and get her on board. That is, if she was still talking to me after what had just happened. I'd have to work on that. I could see I had a lot on my plate now, but it felt good. A path was opening up in front of me.

Just then, the strains of a carol became audible. Both Mr Neale and I stopped to listen. The choir were rehearsing for this afternoon, and their combined voice filtered into the office: 'It came upon the midnight clear . . .'

EMMA

I quickened my pace as I approached the unit. It was bitterly cold; there was an icy frosting on the pavement and the sky was heavy with thick, dull cloud. I was looking forward to getting inside. Mum had dropped me off at the entrance to the hospital as she was late for work, hence this walk through the complex to get to Simon.

A new year, I thought, and who could say what it would bring? At this time last year I wasn't even going out with Simon, then in one year I'd fallen in love and in an instant had it all taken away from me. I scolded myself. That was self-pity, so I resolutely turned my mind from that direction. Like Dan, I was learning to handle this new situation, I was coming to terms with it.

After that incident in the Sixth Form centre, I didn't stay angry with Danny for long. I could understand how he had misinterpreted the whole thing between me and Adam. Thinking back, I was a little foolish. Adam *was* making a play for me, I can see that now. But the funny thing is I would have never let him kiss me if I *had* fancied him. It felt safe precisely because it meant nothing to me. I admit I was taken aback by the force of his kiss under the mistletoe and realised that maybe I shouldn't have got myself in that predicament. I told Dan as much and he said he understood. But to be honest, I'm not even sure if he heard me. He was so full of his new idea.

I smiled to myself as I crossed the road that served the hospital and turned down the hill leading to the unit. Dan was intending to complete this Three Peaks Challenge all by himself. He'd worked out his target was to raise in the region of eighteen thousand pounds. I told him that was ridiculous; he countered by saying it was what Simon needed if he was to get a car, a lightweight wheelchair and various other things. I told him I'd help in any way possible. He also insisted I didn't tell Simon. I said I couldn't see how we could possibly keep it secret as he needed publicity to attract sponsors. Dan said we'd try our best to keep a lid on it, at least in the beginning.

I guess he wanted to surprise Simon and I could understand that. But thinking over what Danny had said, I could see he also felt that it was embarrassing for Simon. It turned him into a thing that you raise money for, a kind of charity, a passive object. It's like on Comic Relief nights, when they intersperse the comedy with footage of starving children so that you feel sorry for them. They tug at your heartstrings. As far as possible, Dan doesn't want to sentimentalise Simon and turn him into a figure of pity, or someone for whom you can salve your conscience by making a donation. Maybe that's the price we'll have to pay for raising money, but if it is, then all the more reason why Simon shouldn't know about it. That was the gist of what he told me, and I really appreciated that. This is the funny thing about Dan – for all his bluster and his ability to lose his temper, he has a sensitive side. A very sensitive side.

All this was in my head as I arrived at the unit. It was good to get inside. Not only because it was warm, but because I'd grown used to the place. I knew the nurses and the SCIs that popped in for physio or just to maintain contact. SCIs are Spinal Cord Injured – the unit was a whole little world and it had its own language. I more or less knew it now – I was on the inside. I'd been here so often since that very first visit, when I could hardly bear to look at Simon, that everything had become normal, and the traction, drips, catheters – all of that, didn't bother me. So much so, that when people on the outside said, 'How dreadful! How good of you to visit him so regularly!' I hardly knew what they meant. It wasn't as bad as you think.

One of Simon's doctors was coming towards me and gave me a cheery wave. I smiled back. The mother of one of the men in the unit – Omar, a T7 incomplete – passed me on the stairs and we said hello. T7 is a thoracic vertebra, lower down than Simon's. The higher up it is, the worse it is. Christopher Reeve's break was C2 complete, higher than Simon's, and that's why he'd needed a ventilator. You can have a complete or incomplete injury. With incomplete you might regain some movement or sensation. Simon's injury is complete.

I said hello to the nurses and asked them if they'd had a good New Year. Tracey said she still had the hangover to prove it. They introduced me to Shirley, an agency nurse who was replacing Mo, who was off with flu. I asked how Simon was today and Tracey grinned at me. 'Go and look for yourself,' she said. That's when I knew something was up. I turned on my heel and made for his ward.

I could see immediately. The halo traction had gone and so had the drip. His head was free. I ran over to him. I babbled on about not knowing this was going to happen, and did he know, and did it feel odd? Simon said it did, his head felt very light, and he still couldn't move it much. But it was a step forward, and I knew what he meant. I felt full of optimism – he was making progress.

Apparently they had only just taken it off that morning. I was the first to see him like this. Even his mother didn't know. I asked him if I could text Dan and he said sure. We discussed his symptoms – he was still getting those spasms in his leg. It was weird – every so often his leg would jerk or move up, as if he was moving it, but he wasn't. They were talking about controlling the spasms with drugs. Simon joked, yet more drugs. He was on all sorts of things and that's why he couldn't have any alcohol. Yet.

He asked me about my New Year. I told him all about Steph's party in as much detail as I could – I'd learned that

Si didn't want to talk about himself all the time – and then how I'd spent the last couple of days doing all the schoolwork the teachers had set for the holidays. And guess what, I told him, guess who had called round to revise for the Politics module? Dan.

'Dan? Working?' Simon asked incredulously.

'Uh huh,' I nodded, and explained there'd been a change. Apparently Mr Neale had got through to him, I said, conscious of keeping back Dan's secret. Simon looked really pleased, and said that if Dan set his mind to it, he'd probably do better than all of us. I asked him why, in that case, had Danny been such a slacker? Simon said he reckoned he was frightened of failure, and if you're frightened of failing, sometimes it's easier not to try.

It was lovely, just sitting and chatting with Simon. I took his hand and tried exercising his fingers, which still weren't obeying all the commands he sent them. But the doctors were optimistic that in time his hands would work after a fashion, although he might have problems doing up buttons, things like that. I asked Simon whether he'd seen all the DVDs we'd bought him for Christmas – our gang had clubbed together and bought him half a dozen. We chatted about them, until we were interrupted by a shout.

'Aren't you coming to say hello to me, then?'

It was Pete. I excused myself from Simon and popped over to his bed. Simon shouted over that he'd seen Pete for the very first time only yesterday. Pete was sitting up and they'd put him in a chair and wheeled him round.

'How weird!' I exclaimed. 'Like, you two are such mates but you've only just met face to face!'

'Too right,' said Pete. 'He's not as good-looking as I thought. Tell you what, Emma, you'd be better off with me. Gis a kiss, love.'

I laughed and pecked him on the cheek.

'Again, again!' he called out.

'Watch it, Emma!' Simon shouted.

I passed Pete over the paper on his bedside table and asked him how he was. 'All the better for seeing you,' he told me. I was beginning to feel embarrassed. I knew there was nothing in it because I'd met his wife and everything, but Pete was one of those men who was always flirting. He teased the nurses, told risqué jokes, the lot. But Simon really liked him, even though they were completely different. I suppose Simon and I could have resumed some kind of physical relationship, but the problem was, there wasn't any privacy. And neither of us liked the idea that people were watching. So we'd never even really kissed – properly – since the accident. It was easier not to think about that side of things at all. Maybe that was why Pete's flirting kind of bothered me, I don't know.

On my way back to Simon's bed, Tim came in – the one they call Tiny Tim, the support worker. He's a huge bloke, probably over six foot without his chair. His injury was twelve years ago. He was abroad on holiday and dived into the swimming pool without checking the depth. T3 complete. But now he competes in the Paralympics and works part-time in the unit.

He greeted us both and parked his chair at the end of Simon's bed.

'So you're out of traction!' he said. 'Nice one.'

'Yeah,' Simon said.

'There'll be no stopping you now. I was just popping in to tell you there's someone coming in later who I think you'd like to meet.'

We were both interested.

'Steve Greenaway – mate of mine, I told you about him. Plays wheelchair rugby.'

There was a flash of interest in Simon's eyes. 'Will you bring him up here?'

'I sure will.'

'Did you have a good New Year?' I asked Tim.

'Not bad. I've got my new website up and running. We had a family party on New Year's Eve at my place.'

Tim has a flat of his own, Simon had told me. He's totally independent. His parents and brothers and sister live nearby, but he never wanted to live with them. He was twenty-four at the time of his accident and he'd told us the last thing he wanted was to go back to being a dependent. Simon had also told me there was a rumour that one of the physios fancied him. She was always being ribbed about it and

Simon reckoned it was true. Tim was good-looking: spiky hair, deep brown eyes with strong, muscly forearms like a lot of the wheelchair-users.

'How about you, Emma? Starring in any new plays?'

I shook my head. The amateur dramatic group I belonged to was in the middle of producing *Fiddler on the Roof*, but I'd never auditioned. The auditions were just after Simon's accident. I said, 'If there's something happening at school, I might.'

'Do it,' Tim said. 'I'd like to come and see you.'

Simon said, 'I'd like that, Em.'

Simon insisted that I get on with my life. He said his injury shouldn't hold *me* back as well. When we'd had that conversation, I told him I was quite happy just being by his side, but he got angry. He said he didn't want me missing out because of him.

And sitting there with Simon that day, with Tiny Tim, and Pete in the next bed, for the first time, I felt the beginning of hope. There was going to be a future for us – a different kind of a future, but a future. I would still be on the stage, Simon would still be playing rugby, and he too would have his own flat and parties and—

'Simon!'

It was Sylvia. She'd just arrived that moment.

SIMON

She notices immediately the halo traction has gone and, apologising to Em, Tim and Pete, she starts asking me whether it hurt when it came off, what the doctors said? She looks at me lying on the bed and comments that I look like a baby lying there. She laughs at her own joke and Emma laughs too, but looks uneasy.

Emma and my mum have always got on, but they both observe each other carefully. Mum wants Emma to like her, but also she's just a tiny bit suspicious of Emma and wonders about our relationship. Emma says she likes Mum, but they've never spent any time alone together, even since I've been in the unit. I've told Emma a lot about Mum, all the old stuff. I thought it might help her understand the way she is.

Mum's in a prattling mood today, taking some old clothes of mine for washing and substituting some new ones. She carries on saying that getting back on my feet is a bit like growing up all over again. She says, 'When you're a baby you can't support your own head for a while, then the next stage is sitting up, then pulling yourself up, crawling, and then . . . Well,' she says, 'it's almost the same.'

Tiny Tim says he has to get on and pushes himself off. Pete starts reading his paper earnestly. Mum asks Emma how she is and she says she's been working hard. Mum asks her if she's thought about applying to drama school yet, or whether she's going to apply after university. Emma replies she'll have to put her mind to deciding soon. I just listen to them. I'm picking up that Mum's prattling, her bright cheeriness, is a front. There's something false about her. Middle height, with untidy short blonde hair with a touch of grey, she takes off her winter coat and lies it on the rail at the foot of my bed. She glances around the ward nervously. Her smile brave, her air distracted.

Emma says she'd better be going and I want to ask her to stay, but this sense that something's up with my mum persists and makes me hesitate. Mum doesn't ask her to stay either. Nor does she move back to let Emma kiss me goodbye. So, awkwardly, Emma smiles, waves goodbye, picks up her jacket and goes, saying things about the weather to cover her embarrassment.

Once she's gone Mum still fusses, asking about my spasms, my drugs, and how I'm getting on with my catheter. I brush off these questions. That leads to a pause, which turns into a heavy silence.

'What's up?' I ask.

'Nothing,' she says resolutely. 'Nothing you need be bothered with.'

I sigh. 'Just because I'm stuck in this bed doesn't mean you can't tell me what's wrong.'

'You have enough to deal with,' she says.

'So maybe I want a break?' I carry on pushing her. I don't know why I do this. If it's about Dad, I don't want to hear what's wrong. But also I want to know the worst; no one likes worrying. And it might not be about Dad. Maybe it's something I can help with, and that would make me feel good. The problem with being an SCI is that you feel so useless a lot of the time. Doing something for someone else helps that feeling go away.

'What's happened, Mum?' I say. 'Please tell me.'

She lowers her voice, so Pete can't hear. 'Honestly, Simon, it's nothing. It's more something that's been building up.'

I question, 'Dad?'

'So you've noticed too?'

'Well, no, but explain.'

'It's nothing, but – oh, I feel he's cut himself off from us. I do understand, I think. In the beginning he was marvellous, almost like he used to be, but then, I think it was once the doctors said you'd never walk again, he just gave up. He was your dad, but he felt he couldn't fix it, he couldn't fix you. And he gave up and just withdrew. Have you noticed he doesn't always come here with me?'

I may be crippled, but I'm not blind. I bite my tongue, and say instead, 'But someone's got to look after David.'

'It isn't that. David's fine, anyway. He's taken the whole thing in his stride. He also cuts himself off, but kids do that – they live in their own little world. It's his way of coping.'

'Maybe that's all Dad is doing.'

I say that because I know what she's thinking. A few years ago – three years ago, to be exact – Mum found out that Dad was seeing someone, a woman in his office. It was a bad time, a very bad time. They talked about divorce but it never came to that, mainly because of me and David. Mum lost loads of weight and was on antidepressants for a while. Dad was desperately unhappy. He told me he never meant it to happen, it was like he couldn't help himself, like some kind of madness took him over. Now he'd come to his senses he would never do anything like that again.

Mum told me it reflected on her attractiveness as a woman and pointed to things that were wrong in their relationship. She said although she was taking him back it would take her years to trust him again, if she ever did. She cried a lot – and that was the part I didn't like. Both of my parents talked to me because they thought I understood better than anyone else what we were all going through. They wanted to keep it in the family. They also wanted a witness of what they were suffering. That was me. That was my role.

I don't think I honestly minded. I listened, and then I got onto the rugby pitch and forgot all about it, or I'd go for a run and run it off. So I let them do it. I felt flattered. I wanted us to be a happy family, and I reckoned it was up to me to make that happen. Like, that year, I won the school prize for academic achievement and they both came together to prize-giving, and looked so proud.

That was history now, and recently more than ever the focus had been on me. There were my GCSEs, and that all went very well. Then my parents were talking about Oxford or Cambridge, and I was thinking of playing rugby for the national squad. And while all that was going on, I had my accident.

'He's been working very long hours, Simon,' my mother says, seeking reassurance.

'Maybe he needs to.'

'Not over the holidays. Either he's avoiding me, or there's more to it.'

'Have you spoken to him?'

'No,' she says. Then her face falls, and she looks close to tears. 'I shouldn't have said any of this to you. Anyway, it's only me being neurotic. I'm sure there's nothing in it. Just delete everything I said from your mind. Okay?'

'Okay.'

'Now listen. Have you had enough physio? Do you want me to exercise you?'

I said I was fine. I knew that my mum would feel better now, just having spoken. I felt sorry for my dad too, and that familiar, churned-up feeling I used to have three years ago came flooding back. It's made up of shame and panic and a desperate desire to make things better. Only now I was totally powerless.

'I'm sorry,' my mum says again. 'It's just that I bottle things up. But do you know, Simon, I've been thinking. It dawned on me the other day that none of this means you can't go to university. Even if you can't manage school, we could get tutors and you could take your A Levels. Then you could go to a local university. I could take you every day. And you could still get a degree. Or even, degrees.'

She sounds triumphant, and this idea chases away the gloom that was clouding her face before. So I don't want to spoil it. I agree; I say that would be great and I can't wait to get back to studying. I tell her about Dan working again and she says she's glad. She always thought it was a great pity he never achieved his potential. 'His mother,' she says, 'will be very pleased indeed.'

She carries on, chatting about this and that. She seems calmer now, a little tired too. I tell her I'm fine and she can go, that Dan is coming later. She seems grateful and prepares to go. She bends over me. 'I can't wait to have you back home,' she says. 'It'll be like old times.' She kisses me and, in a moment or two, she's gone.

I lie there thinking about what she's told me. I don't for one minute think Dad's having an affair again. Not for one minute. But I do think Mum is coping less well than I thought. She's stressed and hassled with all the visiting and now she's imagining things. I don't really see what I can do to help her, except get into proper rehab as quickly as I can.

'Couldn't help overhearing,' Pete shouts across.

I feel myself redden. Did he hear all that stuff about my dad? I hope not. The only person I'd ever told about that was Emma. Even Danny was in the dark about it.

'Nosy git,' I call back.

'Yeah,' he says. 'Now, me, I only got three GCSEs and then an apprenticeship. But what I do know is this: you can go to any uni you like. They have special rooms and that. Facilities for the disabled. I was talking to a girl here, down in the pool room. Incomplete T3. She went on to take a degree two hundred miles away from home. She managed. Your mum means well, but it's up to you in the long run.'

I look down at my thin, useless body, bolstered with pillows and props. I think about the bowel routine the nurses are teaching me and all that business with the catheter – which would be easy, if I could move my fingers properly. I'll need my mum, I'll need some kind of support. And it was looking like she still needs me.

A wave of utter exhaustion washes over me. Everything is so bloody difficult. And I thought once the traction was off, it would be the beginning of the end. I couldn't be more wrong.

'Oy, Simon,' Pete called again. 'Look up!'

I did. There were two flies on the ceiling.

'Mine's the one on the left,' Pete shouted. 'Bet you mine flies off first.'

'You're on,' I say, cheering up. I stare at the flies, willing mine to go. *Come on*, I mouth urgently. *Do it. Make your bid for freedom.* Pete's fly crawls a centimetre or two. Mine was stock still, like someone had painted it on the ceiling.

'You've got no chance,' Pete said. 'Mine's getting ready to charge. Look at him go, go, go!'

And then, all of a sudden, my fly darts away and buzzes across to the far wall. Yesss!! I fill with jubilation. He's done it. He's gone.

'Exactly *how much* do you owe me?' I ask Pete.

DANNY

It was the weather that decided me – blue skies, hardly any clouds, diamond-bright winter sunshine. So I took the bus that went past the hospital and travelled right to the end of the route. It was okay, Simon wasn't expecting me. I was supposed to be learning for a test essay, but I'd have enough time to do that later tonight, I reckoned. This Sunday afternoon I thought I'd just take a walk.

The bus terminated at Ash Edge, a one-street village of blackened stone cottages with three pubs and a chippy. I knew that just beyond it was the Edge itself, a hill that overlooks our town, a shoulder of moorland that broods darkly above us. I'd never been up it. But today was the day.

The thing was, I thought I'd prove to myself that I could do this Three Peaks Challenge. I wanted to see what it would be like, climbing mountains. Well, okay, Ash Edge isn't exactly a mountain, it's a large hill. But then, this is Great Britain, right, not the Himalayas. Our mountains are just basically very large hills. You walk up them until you get to the top.

I was feeling good that afternoon, as I found the footpath that led to the path that wound up to the summit. So far

Simon hadn't got wind of what I was planning to do. Neale had warned me he might very well find out, but he appreciated that I wanted to get the whole thing underway first.

I'd told Neale that I wanted to do the whole challenge by myself. He'd looked very doubtful, and said I might want to reconsider that – the Three Peaks was generally a team effort, for safety reasons if nothing else. But I'd told him this Challenge was something *I* wanted to do for Simon – just me, and me alone. Emma had said something interesting – she'd said it was like I wanted to go through what Si was going through, having a physical ordeal. She might even be right. But that afternoon, it didn't feel at all like an ordeal. There was sunshine, a keen breeze whipping past me – and me, in my parka and new trainers (a Christmas present from Mum and Dad).

An old bloke and his wife approached me in the other direction. They'd probably been to the summit – and if two old wrinklies could do it, it would be a cinch for me. They said a cheery hello and I responded in kind. Then I got my Walkman out of my pocket and put on some decent sounds.

There was a sign that pointed to the path, and I had to go over a stile. No sweat. I climbed over easily and jumped down to the other side, and found myself walking along the side of a field. Now I could feel the rise upwards. On one side of me was a dry-stone wall, on the other some sheep huddled in the distance, balls of dirty cotton-wool on stick legs. I was getting warm now and unzipped my parka. I noticed the trainers were rubbing at the back.

I came to a gate which needed unbolting, and I carefully bolted it again, remembering something about a country code and not letting animals escape or get eaten or something. Whatever. Now I was following a steep path with a drop on one side. I can't say I'm that fond of heights so I kept my eyes ahead of me. I could hear myself breathing and could feel the effort my legs were making. My forehead was damp with the effort. I looked up to see when this ascent would end. It was hard to tell as the path curved, but it didn't look too far. Funny how going uphill is so much effort. The ground comes up to reach your feet, but it's still damn hard work.

I reached the top and looked round. The path curved and stretched up to another summit – so I wasn't there yet! I felt tired, fed up, and wondered if the rubbing at the back of my trainers meant I was getting a blister. There were some clouds ahead now, nothing too serious. I stopped for a while to give myself a rest. I zipped up my parka again. It was getting chilly. Yet despite that, I would have killed for a drink. Stupid of me not to think of bringing some water. My mouth was sticky and my throat felt tight. All the provisions I had was some chewing gum in my pocket. I took a stick of that.

The path was not only steep now, but rock-strewn. I had to watch my footing. I was having to avoid stones and also muddy patches churned up by walkers' boots. I found myself skirting round puddles, leaping from clump to clump of hardened mud or stones. I slipped, and soaked my trainers in some brown gunge. I swore loudly and carried on climbing, my heart pounding and my chest tight with the effort. But I could see in front of me that I'd nearly reached the top. It would be worth it after all.

The top – but no, it wasn't the top. To my right there was open moorland that continued ascending. Was that right? Was I going the right way? There were more clouds now: dull, heavy, thick and grey. Where did they come from? The backs of my heels were killing me. But resolutely I turned and trudged through the grass, stepping on pellets of sheep shit, onwards and upwards.

It was bloody hard work. I was panting with the effort and my leg muscles were aching. I could hardly lift one foot in front of the other. The music in my headphones wasn't helping so I stopped and took my Walkman off. While I was doing that a couple of walkers came up from behind me, greeted me, and walked on, going at twice the rate I'd been going. Who were they? Professional mountaineers or something? What was wrong with me that I couldn't go at that pace?

I pressed on. They were soon completely out of sight. Part of me wanted to turn back, I'd had enough. But surely I must get to the top soon. And I thought I'd got there, but – shit! – the path turned again up a steep, stone-littered path . . . or paths. There were two of them, one climbing steeply and the other going off to the left, more gently. Which one should I take?

I stood scratching my head. What was that on my face? Raindrops? Bugger! I looked above me, saw the two walkers who were ahead, and worked out I had to take the less steep of the two paths. But it was still pretty hard going. I found I was climbing more slowly now, like an old man. It was raining properly and I kept my eyes glued to my feet, which were feeling horribly damp. Either the rain or the mud had got inside my trainers.

The couple ahead of me had turned and were coming down. 'Pretty misty up there,' they told me. I thanked them and pressed on. But they were right. The visibility was getting worse. I jumped out of my skin as a deep, unearthly cry vibrated around me. The Hound of the Baskervilles? No, just a sheep, that was all. A frigging sheep. I put the hood of my parka up over my head, put my hands in my pockets – why hadn't I brought gloves? – and soldiered on.

Five minutes later and I'd had enough. The rain was battering the ground; my face was freezing but I was hot with effort; my feet were blistered; and I didn't have a clue how far the summit was, or whether I'd passed it, or whether I was even going to survive this. So I turned and began my descent, except I could only see a little way in front of me.

Going downhill should have been easier, I thought, but

after a while the backs of your calves start aching with the effort. And then my foot caught on a stone and I went flying. A searing pain shot through my ankle. I scrambled onto one leg, not wanting to rest on the sodden ground. I held my ankle and wondered what the hell I was going to do now. I have to admit, I was beginning to panic. Because of the rain and because it was getting late, darkness was coming quickly. I would have shouted for help but I was pretty sure no one was going to come to my rescue – except maybe that sheep if I was lucky.

But, miraculously, after a time, the pain in my ankle receded and I found I was able to walk. I worked out that if I made sure I kept going down I was bound to come out somewhere civilised. I was sopping wet, cold, miserable, hungry and feeling very, very stupid.

It was already twilight by the time I reached Ash Edge village. The wind had blown the hood of my parka off several times, and my rain-drenched hair was plastered to my head. I was so cold and wet it wasn't true. And, to cap it all, the chippy wasn't open. I returned to the bus stop, but there was no bus and no timetable to tell me when there would be another. I got out my phone – no signal.

And I was the person who reckoned on doing the Three Peaks Challenge by himself – three mountains in twenty-four hours *and* I'd been stupid enough to tell everyone about it! Well, I would just have to un-tell them. I'd find something easier to do to raise money for Simon . . . a sponsored football watch – five games in twenty-four hours? I was joking to myself to hide a disappointment so huge it threatened to engulf me. I'd been living for weeks with the dream of becoming some sort of superhero for Simon, and I'd basically been kidding myself. I couldn't even climb Ash bloody Edge.

I didn't do any learning for the test essay because I wasn't feeling too good when I got home. But it didn't matter, because I missed it – I was off school for a few days with some kind of flu-type virus. It meant I had to pass on seeing Simon, but I managed to croak at him down the phone once or twice.

I got back to school on the Friday, and made it to assembly. The Sixth Form was squeezed into the sides and back of the hall and the whole school listened to the Head read something suitably moral and give a few announcements. Wilko was muttering something about a party at the weekend and was I coming? But I wasn't listening to him or the Head. I was going over what I was going to say to Mr Neale to explain why I'd dropped the idea of the Three Peaks Challenge. But how do you say you don't think you're up to something without sounding like a loser? *Let's face it, Harrison*, I said to myself, *you* are *a loser. Big time.*

The Head shuffles a few papers at the podium, calls up some shiny-faced kids to receive certificates. Then puts down his papers and announces that Daniel Harrison from 6E is undertaking the Three Peaks Challenge some time in June, in aid of the Simon Denham Benefit Fund, and he will be seeking sponsorship from everyone in the school. His eyes seek me out and he beams at me over his horn-rimmed specs. Everyone turns and stares. I turn beetroot. I don't think I've ever been more embarrassed in my whole life. So I study the front of my shoes and see how the laces are slightly frayed at the ends. My mind is still made up. I'm dropping the whole thing.

We headed out of the hall and I made my way back to the Sixth Form centre to get my bags. I became aware of someone running to catch me up. I turned, and there was that fat kid from Year Seven, the one who spoke to me in the library shortly after Simon's accident.

'Danny?' he said, puffing and panting. I thought he sounded vaguely asthmatic. 'Can I go with you?'

'Who are you?' I asked.

'Calvin Whelan,' he puffed. 'Can I? Do the Three Peaks with you?'

'Yeah, whatever,' I grinned. 'It'd be good to have some company.'

'Brilliant,' he said, beaming from ear to ear. 'I'll make loads of money, you won't regret it, honest.'

I nodded and smiled at him. It was mean of me, I know, but since I wasn't going to do it anyway it hardly mattered. Calvin – what a name! Did his parents call him after the underpants? I'd let him have a morning of reflected glory, then I'd find him at break and tell him the whole thing was off and apologise. Meanwhile I passed the Geography room where Mr Neale was talking to another of the Geography teachers. He came out and greeted me.

'Feeling better?' he asked.

I shrugged.

'The Head gave you some good publicity today!'

'Yeah,' I mumbled.

'Aren't you pleased?'

Silence.

'Danny? You haven't gone off the idea?'

He'd been so good to me I felt I owed him an explanation.

'The fact is, I tried to walk up Ash Edge on Sunday and I was knackered. Sorry, exhausted. I couldn't even manage one piddling little hill. How am I going to climb three mountains in twenty-four hours? I was being stupid. Forget it.'

I made as if to leave, but he stood in my way.

'So you're giving up already.'

'Not giving up exactly.'

He frowned as if he didn't understand me.

'I'll do something else to get some money,' I said.

He looked at me through narrowed eyes. 'True, you're not very fit. You could do with losing a stone or two – extra weight makes a difference to stamina levels. You also need to train. Start running or cycling and do it regularly. I'm still rather dubious you ought to attempt the challenge alone. You have no outdoor skills. Can you read a compass? Can you find your way using cairns? Do you have good walking boots? A pole? Crampons?'

'Stop messing around, Sir.'

'But I know someone who does. What you need is an experienced walker to go with you and keep you motivated. Someone who can stop you getting lost and make sure you have the right equipment.'

'Who do I know like that?'

Then the penny dropped. It was the look on Mr Neale's face. Sort of hesitant, pleased – rather embarrassed, to tell you the truth.

'You mean you.'

'How about it? I've climbed a number of mountains and my map-reading skills are second to none.'

This was getting crazier by the minute. It was because the whole thing was so crazy, that I thought: why not? 'Okay,' I said. Mr Neale smiled at me, delighted.

Then I'm thinking: what the hell have I got myself into here? I am not only going to climb Ben Nevis, Scafell and Snowdon in under twenty-four hours with a fitness level of about zero, but accompanied by the Head of Sixth and . . . and . . . podgy Calvin Whelan from Year Seven.

'You won't regret it,' Mr Neale said. 'We'd better get you

training. I'll have a word with the Head of Games and see what he recommends.'

'Sir,' I interrupted, and explained about Calvin. Mr Neale looked thoughtful.

'I don't see why not,' he said. 'It might do him the world of good. Did you know he's been bullied? School's on top of it now, but I think I understand why he wants to get on board with you.' He paused, then looked at me, amused. 'Naturally you know who Calvin Whelan is?'

'Nope,' I said. 'Why should I?'

'Fred Whelan's son.'

'And Fred Whelan is . . .?'

'The owner of Motortunity – only the biggest second-hand car dealership in the region. There are branches everywhere.'

'So he must be loaded, then.'

Mr Neale nodded. 'I think you've just solved our transport problems, Danny. A good morning's work. Now, off to your lessons.'

EMMA

'I thought you said your dad was picking us up?' I asked Danny, as we exited the unit and emerged onto the darkened car park. There was no sign of Danny's dad's Punto.

'He is,' said Dan, 'but not here. We're meeting him at Lee Wood Park.'

'But that's a twenty-minute walk from here!'

'Exactly,' he said, turned, and grinned at me. 'It's part of my training.'

'Come on, then,' I said, grabbing his arm and walking as fast as I could. 'No slacking here.' He laughed and we set off.

Simon had been in an excellent mood. Just that morning they'd let him sit up for a short space of time. He said it made him feel really spaced out, but that was normal. Pete had cheered him on and the nurses had applauded. Simon was talking feverishly about his physio, saying that as soon as he was used to being in the chair, he could get down to the physio room and start exercising his arms. But his fingers were still curled in that odd way. I noticed that. And, once he was off the Warfarin, he told us, he could drink again. 'We'll get leathered, Dan,' he joked.

Dan nodded and stole a glance at me. The fact was, Dan hardly drank any more. He was taking his training very, very seriously. His parents had paid for him to join a gym; he ran some nights and watched what he ate. He'd already lost about ten pounds, I reckoned, and looked a lot better for it. Jen had noticed and had started flirting with him again. She offered to go running with him but, thankfully, he refused. I'm not sure I could have stood Jen falling for Dan all over again!

Dan and I walked silently for a while, alone with our thoughts. The road was busy with visitors and the occasional ambulance. I was glad Si had been so cheerful. But it was funny, now that he was getting to be more and more like the old Simon every day, he also seemed less and less like the old Simon. There was a new person rising from the ashes. The realisation struck me for the first time, and I had to share it with Dan.

'Do you think Simon's changed? I mean, in his character?'

Dan fell into step with me. 'He's got tougher and he's obsessed with getting moving again. But no, not really.'

I said nothing. I felt there *was* a change. He'd become part of the unit, one of the residents there. The life he had there was important to him. It was his only life. As his girlfriend, I knew I had a role to play, but it was just a role. Before his accident, I used to feel as if I was the centre of his life. Now I was on the periphery. But – and this was the hard part to admit – I didn't mind. I preferred it that way. I liked being Simon's best friend, along with Dan. I was almost becoming an honorary bloke. All three of us would sit and chat about school, sport, the latest gossip. I liked that.

'He seems to have got closer to his mum,' Dan broke in.

'Yeah. That's inevitable. He'll be very dependent on her when he gets home.'

'It must be weird. Just when you're moving away from your parents, to suddenly have to have them do everything for you again.'

'And Simon feels so responsible for his parents.'

'Yeah?'

'Yeah. Since his dad's affair.'

'What?!'

'Didn't you know?' I was horrified at my gaffe. I'd always imagined Si had told Dan when it happened. But then I thought about it and realised that Simon would have been too young then, too young to realise it was right to share. He'd have been embarrassed and kept it to himself. Simon had only told *me* a few months ago and then it was easier as my mum divorced my dad years ago, and I was cool with it.

'That's disgusting,' Dan said. He sounded as if he meant it.

I filled him in very briefly and made him promise never to breathe a word to a soul. Dan said he never would; he also said it explained a lot, especially how he'd always felt Simon and his mum were close, unusually close. He reckoned if his dad had done something like that, he'd have also sided with his mother. I've noticed that – boys are protective of their mums. Me and my mum fight like cat and dog sometimes.

We came to the junction where the hospital road met the main road. Yellow street lamps threw a garish light along the dual carriageway. We turned and walked towards Lee Wood Park, which was a leisure park I'd been to a few times. There was a cinema there, a health club, a few chain restaurants, a bowling alley and a large twenty-four-hour Tesco over the road. I was scurrying to keep up with Dan.

'You're walking too quickly,' I said. He apologised and fell back into step with me. I linked arms with him and we made our way along the pavement by the grass verge. The occasional car rushed past; there were few people around. I asked Danny how his training had been going. He laughed.

'Not bad. The hardest part was getting started. First time I went to the gym, there were all these dead-hard blokes lifting weights and staring at me. I felt they could crush me with their little fingers. Then I realised, no one in the gym cares what anyone else is doing. They're just there for themselves. So I go regularly now and it's not bad. But the crazy bit—' He laughed again and his laughter was infectious; I felt myself smiling. 'The crazy bit is going out running with Neale and Calvin. The three of us ran round Ash Valley Park on Sunday afternoon. What a joke! Mr Neale, all six foot two of him, in shorts and baseball cap; little Calvin panting to keep up, his inhaler in his pocket, not able to keep his mouth shut, rabbiting on about anything and everything; and me in the middle.' We were both laughing so much we had to stop walking. 'Neale says it was a bonding exercise.' I held my sides, which ached from laughing.

'It's just the picture of you!' I explained, and tried to calm down.

'Fair enough,' Dan said. 'But that little kid would be all right, if he'd only shut up. He's given me the potted history of every team he supports, gone through his family tree, told me about the bullying, which *was* pretty bad, that they've moved him to another class, how he wants to impress the boys and how there's this girl—'

'But he's only twelve!' I interrupted.

'Kids start early these days,' Dan said. And we were silent for a bit.

I asked him then, 'What's Mr Neale really like – now you're getting to know him?'

'He's all right,' Dan said, as if he was arguing with himself. 'He still comes over as a bit of a teacher at times, but, you know, sometimes it's easier to talk to him than my parents. He's old and that, but I don't feel like he's got all these expectations. He sees me as I am now, not as the kid I was, or the adult they want me to be.'

'You're different now to how you were a few months ago. Simon's accident has changed *you* too.'

We reached Lee Wood Park. An entry road circled its way around the entertainment complex. It was one of those places that you could really only get to by car.

'Where are we meeting your dad?' I asked Danny.

'Outside the AMC,' he said, scanning the traffic. 'But he's not there yet.'

We crossed the road to get to the entrance of the cinema. That was when it happened. That precise moment. I glanced up at him and our eyes met. Something clicked. I thought: I like you, Danny. I like you more than I should. Immediately I squashed the feeling. I was mad – it was because I hadn't had a proper relationship with Simon for so long – I was projecting my feelings for Simon onto Danny. I was just tired and not thinking properly, I'd imagined it, completely imagined it.

We waited outside the cinema, watching people coming in and out. We stood about six inches apart, both of us in jeans and trainers, not touching, but not too far apart. I pushed my hair behind my ears. Then I rubbed my hands together briskly.

'It's cold,' I said.

'Do you want to go inside?' he asked.

'No,' I replied. 'No, it's all right.'

DANNY

But she carried on shivering. And just ten minutes ago I would have warmed her with a hug. But not now, and not ever again. Because, just before, as we were crossing the road, I'd just glanced at Emma – a dead ordinary look, the sort you give someone just to check they're there, that they're with you – and I thought: I fancy her.

No – it was more than fancy. Fancy is what you do to girls you don't know well, girls who turn you on. What I felt for Emma was different. It was more like: here is a person who understands me, who I could really care about. *And* she turns me on. The feeling was terrifying. I also knew it was completely hopeless. Emma belongs to Simon. I repeated that to myself: *Emma belongs to Simon.* Against the odds, she'd stuck by him since the beginning. He depended on her completely. The worst thing I could ever do would be to steal her from him. Not that I could – Emma loved Simon, and always had done. I was Simon's mate and defended his interests. I'd socked Adam for daring to make a move on Emma. 'Jealous?' Adam had suggested. Now, standing in front of the cinema with Emma, I felt the justice of that.

Then, I'm like: what are these stupid thoughts that I'm having? I wanted to strike them dead, annihilate them. I was quiet, very quiet. So was Emma. The silence between us was making me uncomfortable.

'I'm ravenous,' I said suddenly. 'Starving.'

'Get something to eat,' she said.

'I will.' I left her and went over to the popcorn counter and bought a huge carton. I returned to Emma, offered her some: she declined, and then I stuffed handful after handful down me, as fast as I could. 'That's better,' I said, as I ate.

'Don't talk with your mouth full,' she admonished me. That comment cheered me up; it felt more normal. I turned to her and opened my mouth wide, to show her all the popcorn. That'll put her off me, I thought.

'Ewwww!!!' she said. Then, 'Look – isn't that your dad?'

It was. I thought then, what was the point of the walk we'd just had, now that I was stuffing myself with popcorn? But, hey, I'd burn it off tomorrow. I pushed the front seat down, got into the back of the car, and told Emma to get in the front.

Dad said, 'How was Simon?'

'Fine,' we both said together.

EMMA

We both laughed, at the way we answered Dan's dad's question with the same words and the same intonations. 'Fine.' Like we were a couple.

Which we weren't, I told myself. Not now and not ever. I looked straight ahead through the windscreen and told myself that I'd read too much into that moment as we crossed the road. It was late and I was tired. I'd been enjoying chatting with Dan and it had spilled over into a moment of fondness that I'd misread for something else. Jen was the sort of girl who had crushes and two-timed. I'd never had a really serious boyfriend before Simon and I never cheated. But all the time I knew I was lying to myself – I was conscious of Dan's presence in a way that I never had been before. I could feel the space his body was occupying in the back of the car. I was willing him to say something to his dad, not to cover my embarrassment, but just so I could hear the sound of his voice.

No – I was mad, completely mad. I said to myself: *think of Simon, think how much you love him*. I pictured Simon there on his bed, his excitement as he was telling us about sitting up. I thought of his poor thin body, the way his legs lay awkwardly on the bed, and my heart contracted with love and pity. How could I ever, ever, do anything to hurt that boy? He needed me. Okay, so for one moment I fancied Dan. It was an accident; now it's over, and it won't happen again. I'll make sure of that. I thought: tomorrow I'll buy Simon a present. A CD – no, some jewellery. Maybe a ring, a token, something that will bind us together, that'll tell him how much I love him. Because I do. I really do.

SIMON

I'm lying on my bed and my thoughts are going round and round interminably. Nothing new there, but today it feels different, as if there's a conclusion I'm trying to reach. Something's bothering me.

It can't be my rehab, as that's going well. I'm able to do a little more every day. My mum's very positive, always talking about when I get home and the changes that they're already making. They're going to get a ramp built, as there are steps that lead up to our front door that I wouldn't be able to manage. Mum and Dad are looking into an external lift so I can get upstairs, or maybe a stair-lift. They're weighing it all up at the moment. But every time we have those discussions, part of me is, like: *yeah, whatever*.

Maybe I'm scared of leaving here? Maybe I'm still having trouble coming to terms with what's happened? And so my thoughts revolve. Endlessly.

Pete's back. He's been downstairs, working out. He says he's shattered. He's grinning, in a good mood, and we discuss what he's been doing. He says that he might be having a weekend at home soon, if his wife can get things sorted. He tells me his mum's going to have the kids, to make it easier.

'Looking forward to it?' I ask, stating the obvious.

'You bet!' Pete says. Then he makes a rude gesture.

I laugh at him to hide my embarrassment and also realise I've got a chance now to talk about the one thing that's been on my mind more and more lately. 'Can you have normal sex?' I really meant, could *I*?

Pete propels himself over to my bed. 'Normal sex? Depends what you mean by normal. Did I ever tell you about the time . . .?' He sniggers a bit, then looks more serious. 'Well, that's something I'm going to have to find out.' He smiles at me and I'm glad we're having this conversation. It's easier to talk to Pete about this than anyone else. One, he's a cripple like me. Two, because *he's* not awkward with it, I'm not awkward.

'A lot of the blokes here, they use Viagra. That's something I'll be looking into. But to tell you the truth, forget the Viagra – I can't wait to get my hands on my wife!'

'Doesn't it bother you, having to use a catheter all the time? And what if you have an accident – what if your bowels let go or something, when you're in bed with your wife?'

Pete shrugged. 'We'll have to laugh it off, I suppose. Sex is messy at the best of times.'

'But do you ever think, does your wife still fancy you?

You're not like you were when she first met you, or when you married her.'

'Look, Simon, I was there when both of the kids were born, and she's lying on a table with her legs apart, there's blood and whatever, and I probably felt closer to her then than any other time. The last thing I thought about was whether I fancied her.'

I chuckle. Then he said, 'Don't worry. It'll sort itself out.'

But it won't, I think. It's okay for Pete, he's *had* sex, he's been married for ages. He can adjust. But who would want to have sex with me now? I couldn't imagine letting Emma – letting a girl see me as I am. The bloke's supposed to be the one who makes all the moves; he's seductive, irresistible, he puts the girl at ease. And if Emma and I ever get to the point again when she's willing to try, I won't even be able to control my own body. I can't see any other way but to stay a virgin. Because, basically, despite all my progress with my chair and my upper body strength, I'm just a freak. All the others boys will be shagging, and I'll be just listening, and, and . . .

Clumsily, I pick up my headphones and jam them on. It's easy to work the cassette recorder – I've developed the knack of pushing the buttons with the knuckle of my little finger. Then I push the volume button to the loudest possible and use the music to drown my thoughts, blast them out of my head. I like it when the singer shouts and raves, and welcome the mad whine of the guitar. I want to block out everything, especially my knowledge of what I'm going to have to do. Soon. Very soon.

I've reached my conclusion.

Emma's here. I'm surprised, because it's Sunday morning and none of my visitors arrive until just after lunch. She looks happy. Her hair is tied back in a ponytail and her face is clean of make-up. She's wearing a little pink top and jeans. She pulls up a chair to the side of my bed and asks me how I am and we have the usual catch-up chat. I feel nervous. Though I'd been scripting all of this in my head, I wasn't ready now. I didn't expect her yet. It's strange that she should be here now, almost as if she knew.

She takes my hand and holds it. She's being very affectionate today. She leans over and kisses my cheek. She says she has a surprise for me, then changes the subject and tells me about the movie she saw with Steph last night. I'm not listening because I'm not sure how to start saying what I want to say to her.

'I wanted to come early—' Emma says.

'There's something I want to talk about—' I say, but at the exact same time as Emma. We laugh as our words become entangled.

'You first,' I say.

'No, you.'

'You,' I insist.

'Oh, okay.' She takes her bag from its position on the

floor and opens it. 'Give me your hand,' she says. I extend it. She fumbles around and takes out a little package. From the plastic bag she takes out a small box, opens it and removes a gold ring. She places it on my finger.

'I wanted to give you this while we were alone,' Emma says. 'Just to tell you how much I love you.'

My hand lies motionless, unresponsive, by me on the bed. The ring sits on my finger reproachfully. I don't know what to say.

'Simon?' There's a nervous, frightened tone to her voice. This is awful, worse than I thought it would be. Why can't I find the right words? I turn to her.

'Thanks, Em. But, look, I've been wanting . . .'

She doesn't say anything, doesn't help me out.

'I've been wanting to say, you're free, you know. You don't have to keep going out with me. I understand if you want a break. This isn't fair on you.'

'No!' she states, almost as if she's scared. 'No.'

'We can still be friends,' I say. 'I don't know what I'd do if we weren't friends. But you can see other people, if you like. It's fine, you know.'

Tears spring to her eyes and I feel low-down and mean. I'm taken aback, too. Every time I've staged this scene in my head, Emma thanks me and we agree to split. I didn't have a scenario when she *refuses* to break up with me.

She says, 'Have you gone off me?'

'No!' I say. 'Not at all. You know that.'

'Then why . . .?'

I don't want to have to say the next bit, but now I have no choice.

'I'm thinking about the future. When I get out of here, we won't be able to turn the clock back. I'm not going to be able to have normal sex, not without stuff like Viagra.' I feel disgusted as I say the word. It's a dirty old man's drug. When Em and I were going to have sex, it was going to be like on the movies. But there's no plot, no script, no parts for a useless cripple and a gorgeous, normal girl.

'Sex isn't everything,' Emma says.

But I know she's wrong. It might not be everything, but it's the centre, isn't it? It's what a relationship is all about.

'You deserve better than me,' I say, and realise I sound self-pitying. Emma picks up on that.

'No, that's not right. *I* don't deserve *you*! And just because you're injured it doesn't mean you deserve any less. That's ridiculous, Simon, and you know it.'

I sigh. I seem to be losing this and I don't know how I feel about that. I try again.

'I'm a mess, Emma. You won't be able to have the same feelings about me . . . when you see me. I don't just mean the wheelchair and all the devices I'm going to have to use, but half my body is useless. I have to watch my health. If I get pressure sores, or if my bladder's too full, my blood pressure rises and I could even have a stroke.'

I watch Emma's reaction to that. There's just the slightest

pause and I see her gather herself together. She could be on the stage. She has that same air of being conscious of people watching her, a controlled dignity, her head held high.

'All the more reason why you need me,' she says. 'You can't go through all that alone.'

'I have my mother,' I countered, and again I get this thudding feeling of utter despair.

'But you don't want to live with your mother for ever.'

'No, I don't, of course I don't. No, what I'm trying to say is, I don't want you taking all this on. Emma, I love you too much to want you to have to go through this.'

Emma was into her stride now.

'It's because I love you so much that I want to go through this with you, us two together. I'm not so shallow that I care at all about the things you've told me. I'm not some kind of bimbo who only fancies people who are good-looking. I know you, Simon, and that means so much more to me than anything. I want to be by your side!'

'Okay,' I say, as much to stop her speech as anything else. There was something about the way she was talking that made me think she was trying to convince herself as well as me. I feel exhausted with all the emotion.

Then she bends over me and for the first time since my accident she kisses me properly. Her familiar, soft, sweet mouth pushing against mine, our mouths merging, becoming one. But I'm lying prone on my bed and she is taking the initiative. Old feelings stir in me, but at the same time I want her to stop. I feel myself getting aroused and it panics me. My eyes are wide open. Eventually Emma pulls away.

'Please say we can go back to how we were,' Emma says.

'Yeah,' I say. 'It's just that . . . I thought you didn't fancy me any more.'

'No, Si. I think it's more that you don't think of yourself as fanciable.'

Which, I suppose, is true, and it takes a girl to work out that sort of thing. I wonder if I was wrong to have started this conversation. Certainly I feel relieved now, glad we're still together. Glad also that we've been able to talk about sex. Maybe it *will* be all right, I don't know. Who knows?

We hold hands for a bit, not saying anything. I still have a girlfriend. Nothing's changed.

But that's a lie. I have to confront the fact that my accident has changed everything. Mum says it's like I'm a baby again, but that's not true. I feel more like . . . like a pupa – you know, that thing a caterpillar becomes, that white wrapped-up thing, that's waiting to transform into something different. Okay, so maybe I won't turn out as a butterfly. But I will be quite different in the future, and Emma is part of my past. And being with her makes me feel like I ought to be the person I was in the past, the person I can't ever be again.

I don't know if anyone – Emma, Mum, Dad, Dan – if *anyone* understands that.

EMMA

I was trembling a bit, but kept the hand that held Simon's as steady as I could. He mustn't know the turmoil I was going through. He mustn't know how when he offered me my freedom my heart leapt with joy. But only for a second, only for one tiny second. I knew where my duty lay, where I was committed, and what I had to do.

I was hurt, too, that he wanted to finish with me. I thought maybe he'd stopped fancying me. But, no, it wasn't that. He was just going through a low patch. But we'll bounce back up. I do love Simon, I do. Really.

Then I thought, I'd better be going. I didn't want to be there when Dan arrived. So I kissed Simon again, told him I loved him, and both of us felt a bit tearful, but closer than ever, I think, I hope.

DANNY

I started training really hard. In the beginning it was because I didn't want Ash Edge to defeat me again, but after that the training kind of took over. I ran most days, either at the gym, or outdoors if it was fine. I watched the seasons change: I saw March days, uncertain whether they were going to be sunny or not, with a sprinkle of crocuses on the grass verges. Then came the daffodils – I'd never really noticed flowers before – bright yellow trumpets, crowds of them, planted by council workers gone crazy. Next were days when the sun made me warm and I wriggled out of my fleece as I ran. Now it was May, the pavements littered with pink blossom that fell like confetti from the trees. As each month gave way to the next, I got fitter, Simon made more progress, and what seemed so abnormal back in November began to feel normal to all of us. Time passed and, though it didn't exactly heal us, we were no longer in shock. Simon's injury was a fact of life – a fact of his life, my life, Emma's life.

So I ran, I lifted weights, I climbed hills. When I wasn't doing that I badgered people to sponsor me. And when I wasn't doing that, I worked for my exams. So the question of Emma didn't really arise. I wouldn't let it. We were still good mates and it seemed to me she and Simon were closer than ever, like husband and wife almost.

Simon was as obsessed with his training as I was. He was also lifting weights in the gym at the unit, under the watchful eye of an enthusiastic physio. He was stretching, to keep his muscles loose and supple. He was practising transfers and even standing in a standing frame. He was also becoming adept in his wheelchair, so much so that next weekend he was coming home for a visit – his first time since the accident.

Even now, I thought, as I picked up speed – I was on my way to Mr Neale's house for a planning meeting – even now, when I tell people about Simon, their faces are aghast with horror, they mutter something like, 'How dreadful!' and shuffle with embarrassment. But I want to tell them it's not like that any more. Sure, Simon gets his bad days – he turned the air blue when he was struggling to do up the buttons on his shirt – but he's adjusted; we all have. I turned the corner and ran alongside the park. Mind you, if people didn't feel sorry for Simon, I wouldn't be getting so much sponsorship.

I noticed a car overtake me, then slow down. It was a soft-top Mercedes. I smiled to myself and ran up to it. Calvin got out of the car, in navy shorts and a football shirt.

'I knew you'd come this way. I thought I'd join you and do some running. My dad said he'd drop me off. He's meeting us at Mr Neale's later. Bye, Dad, thanks for the lift.'

Mr Whelan beamed at me and drove off. Calvin was jogging on the spot.

'Getting warmed up. You've got to get warmed up because it makes your muscles more flexible. So you don't get toxins in your muscles – that's what causes the cramps. We could run through the park, you know, because there's a hill and we need to get used to ascending hills . . .'

We were off now and he was at my heel, chatting non-stop.

'My dad's trainer took me out running. He said you should keep a steady pace, so you can still talk. Dad's going to take me for a practice climb up Brown Edge Hill next weekend. He's got me one of those satellite navigation systems in case we get lost. Well, I know we won't, but it's ace, Danny. You can tell where you are anywhere in the world. I used it during break yesterday and you could tell from it we were in the school playground . . .'

Calvin was my own personal radio station: Calvin Whelan FM. Sometimes I tuned in to him, but most of the time I was lost in my own thoughts as I ran. Random stuff, mostly. I was thinking that just as people are still so pitying of Simon, they are saying how wonderful it is, what I'm doing. But it's not, not at all. It's just a consequence of what happened to Simon – I'm doing what I have to do, that's all. And, guiltily, I thought: in some ways things are better for me now. I've changed even more than Simon. Well, on the outside.

'Russell's been off school for ages and then they found out his mum had taken him away on holiday without telling the school. Mrs Sutcliffe was livid. At first I thought Tony might be bullying him and I'm glad I was wrong. But listen – the other day, Mark, David's friend, invited me to his party. Not that there'll be girls there or anything. Danny, how old were you when you started going out with girls?'

We started climbing; I tried to increase my pace.

'Danny, how old were you when you started going out with girls?'

'Eight,' I told him. 'By your age I'd lost my virginity ten times over.'

A pause, then he laughed. 'You went out with Jenny Stephenson, didn't you? She's nice. She's pretty – not as pretty as Emma, though. It must be rotten for Emma. I mean, it's worse for Simon, obviously, but she's not having a normal life – I mean, a normal boyfriend . . .'

I started running faster, sprinting, almost. I reckoned Calvin had to stop yakking to keep up with me. But no such luck – he was getting fitter by the day.

'Do you fancy Emma, Danny?'

'Nah, she's a dog,' I joked.

'You're kidding,' he said. 'Brent Smith in my class fancies her, but he keeps it quiet because he sits next to David.

David's got friendly with these boys in Year Eight: James Whittington, Tony Melton . . .'

I tuned out. What Calvin had said about Emma hadn't bothered me at all. Not one little bit. I was completely over her. Even that dream I had the other night – the one that stayed with me all day and meant I couldn't look her in the eyes when I thought about where my subconscious had taken me – even that had almost gone. I was even able to joke about her. I wasn't even bothered that there was this kid in Year Seven that fancied her. Cheek of it. I never fancied anyone in the Sixth Form when I was in Year Seven. Who did he think he was?

Anyway, I told myself, the last thing I would ever do is come between Simon and Emma now. They were meant for each other, everyone knew that. Their relationship was kind of sacred, in a way. Yeah, sacred.

We turned out of the park gates and slowed down as we jogged along the road that led to Mr Neale's turning. Mr Neale. Robert Neale. He'd said, 'Enough of this Mr Neale rubbish; when we're training or planning, call me Robert.' Now that was seriously weird. Calling a teacher by their first name was the nerdiest, creepiest thing ever. I'd nodded, agreeing I would, but knowing it was never going to happen.

I'd seen his house before – Dad dropped him off once when he picked us up from climbing in Derbyshire. I'd never actually been inside. But Mr N said there were lots of things to go through and discuss, and it was better left to the weekend when we could all get together out of school.

Calvin's dad's car was already parked in the drive. We rang the doorbell and Mr Neale was there to greet us. He ushered us into the front room. I don't know what I expected it to look like. I suppose, if I'm honest, like an extension of the Geography room, but of course it was an ordinary living room: big telly, green fabric sofa, a cabinet with some ornaments on, and some framed photos. I glanced at those because I was interested in his wife. After Mr Neale excused himself, saying he'd get some maps, I noticed a photo that had to be of her. Both she and Mr Neale were sitting together at a table in front of a café. Neale's hair was wavy then and reached his collar. Mr Uncool. I couldn't help smiling. But it was his wife I wanted to look at properly. Her head was resting on his shoulder. She had short, curly hair and was laughing. Mr Neale looked really happy. I thought: life is so damn unfair.

Next thing, the door opens and two kids walk in: a little girl around eight or so, and a boy of about five. They looked at me, Calvin, and Calvin's dad; the girl giggled a bit, and the boy said, 'Are you going to climb those mountains with my daddy?' Before I could answer, I heard a woman call the children away. I reckoned Mr Neale had got his mum in to look after the kids so we could concentrate on the matters in hand.

Before too long Mr Neale was back with us and in full planning mode. Teachers kill me. They really get a kick out of talking and telling you what to do. He spread out these maps on the floor and began explaining to us that we had to decide every detail of the routes beforehand. He said that although the Three Peaks was a question of stamina and fitness, it also depended on timing. We had to start ascending Ben Nevis in the evening and get down before it got too dark. Then we had to drive to Scafell, about four hours or so down the M6, and start climbing again at dawn. With luck on our side, we should be down for breakfast, back in the car and off to Snowdon, getting up there around midday, and then we should finish in plenty of time.

'But Sir,' Calvin said, putting his hand up.

Mr Neale said, 'It's okay, we're not in school.' I caught him smiling to himself.

'But Sir, which path are we going to use to climb Snowdon? There are lots of different ones, aren't there? There's the Pyg Trail, the Llanberis path, the Miners' Track and—'

'You're quite right. Come and look at this OS map.' He gestured Calvin to come and join him on the floor, where the map was spread out. They pored over it, heads close together. They were having a great time and again I felt a twinge of uneasiness. Simon's accident had led to this – to all these people having fun, planning the adventure of a lifetime. It seemed wrong, and yet I was beginning to see how mixed-up life was, how good things lead to bad things, and bad things to good things, and nothing was ever plain and simple. Like, if there was a girl you liked, really liked, and you thought she might like you too—

Mr Neale got to his feet. 'So much for routes,' he said. 'Now what about transport?' We all looked at Calvin's dad.

We knew he'd been invited to this meeting as he wished, in his own words, to make us an offer we wouldn't want to refuse.

Mr Whelan cleared his throat. 'You'll need a decent motor. Something big enough for you all to stretch out in and have a nap. So I'll let you have a Galaxy for the day, petrol included. No charge. Who's driving?'

I spoke up then. 'My dad's offered,' I said.

'Look,' said Mr Neale. 'I have a better idea. What about asking Simon's parents?'

'But we've kept the whole thing from Simon!' I said. 'I wanted to surprise him.'

'I know, but not everyone likes surprises. And just as the Challenge is giving you a focus and the chance to help Simon, don't you think his parents would like that too?'

It was irrational, but I didn't want them. But you can't always have exactly what suits you, and I could see the justice in what Neale was saying. Still, I'd properly gone off Simon's dad after what Emma had told me.

'Okay,' I said.

'Good!' said Mr Neale in that voice he used to use when we got a question right in class. 'I'll have a word with them. They're coming into school on Monday to discuss Simon starting again next year. And how's the sponsorship shaping up, Danny?'

I told him. So far I'd got pledges amounting to three thousand six hundred pounds from kids in the school and people I know. It was good, but not good enough. Mr Neale said his total was running at one thousand seven hundred pounds. Calvin put up his hand again.

'It's all right, Calvin,' Mr Neale said. I saw Mr Whelan smile at his son indulgently.

'What I did, Sir and Danny,' Calvin explained, 'was to write to the Rugby Union and they've pledged money, and Dad said you should ask big stores like the supermarkets and cinema chains, and also Dad's on the board of the City team, and we contacted all the players, and . . .' There was a pause. I'm a bit taken aback. He'd been talking non-stop to me on all of our runs, but hadn't told me any of this. 'And my pledge total,' he piped up, 'is ten thousand, eight hundred and thirty-two pounds, and sixty-three pence.'

'Sixty-three pence?' I asked.

'Yes,' Calvin said. 'The kids at my sister's nursery are giving their spending money.'

We'd done it! We'd be able to afford a car for Simon and more besides. Only it was Calvin's work, not mine. That geeky little kid had done all of this. I just wished it had been me, that's all. But, hey, the most important thing was that we were going to get the money. All we had to do now was complete the Challenge. Mr Neale was carrying on with the planning.

'Apart from a driver, we could do with someone who could prepare some hot food – it's a lot better for walking on – the more calories, the better. Danny – it's about time you bought yourself some decent walking boots – you'll need to wear them in, so they won't give you blisters. Minimum equipment will comprise: waterproofs, emergency whistle, emergency rations, a torch, maps – the weather can be pretty grim on the top of Ben Nevis, even in the height of the summer.'

Listening to Mr Neale sort of cheered me up. The money wouldn't be ours unless we completed the Challenge. There was still work to do. I also began to think of what Simon's reaction would be. It was probably just as well that he found out now. Once he was home next weekend it would be almost impossible to keep our plans from him. Up till now, it had been relatively easy to have a word with all his visitors. Now that the Challenge was only six weeks away, we'd be pushing our luck.

Once again the door to the front room opened, and Mr Neale's little girl appeared, irresistibly attracted by our presence. She stood there, simpering.

'Come in, Lucy,' Mr Neale said. She ran over to her dad

and stood by him, clearly wanting to be part of things, but far too shy to make a move. She whispered something to Mr Neale. Next, her brother shot in. Cute kids, both of them.

'Lucy? Michael?' came that female voice again. A woman of about Mr Neale's age entered – not his mother after all. 'Are the kids bothering you, Rob?' she asked.

'No, we've finished now. Juliet, I'd like you to meet Danny Harrison – you've heard a lot about him – and Calvin Whelan, and his dad, Fred.'

Juliet? Who was she?

'This is Juliet,' Mr Neale continued, 'my fiancée.'

I was shocked. I couldn't help looking again at the photo on the side, of Mr Neale with his wife. She was so pretty and childlike, almost. This Juliet was totally different: rather plump, with dark shaggy hair and big specs.

'I'm hoping to bring the kids to meet you all, when you get down from Snowdon,' she said, in a faint Geordie accent.'

'Great,' I replied.

She offered us drinks, and tore a strip off Mr Neale for not having thought to offer them before. Funny to see one of your teachers being told off. So we made lots of polite chit-chat, and for once I was glad that Calvin Whelan could bore for Britain. I wanted some time to think. There was stuff that was bothering me, to do with Mr Neale's fiancée. Maybe Mr Neale was just marrying this Juliet so the kids could have a mother. He couldn't love her, not like he did his wife. I wondered if Juliet was okay with that, just being second-best? Did they ever talk about his first wife together? Did they feel guilty? Would his kids feel, when they grew up, that he'd betrayed their mum?

Or did people just move on?

SIMON

I'm pushing myself out of the main corridor, into the lobby, and here I am, outside, my dad's car waiting. It's a warm sunny day, but I don't really take in much of what's around me. One thought fills my head: I'm going home. I hardly slept last night, like a kid before Christmas. Mum's promised me a home-made steak pie and then some lemon meringue – no more hospital food. Well, at least for the weekend.

Dad and Tracey are busy setting up the sliding board and with their guidance I ease myself onto it. I can just about shuffle along and soon I'm sitting in the front seat of my dad's car. I've done it. Everyone's cheerful, joking, strapping me in; Tracey's folding my chair and they're putting it in the back of the car; Pete's outside in his chair shouting comments. Dad slams the door then jumps into the driver's seat. It's ten o'clock Saturday morning, and I don't have to be back at the unit until Sunday night.

I am just so glad to be driving away from the unit, out of the hospital, that I don't even want to talk. I take a deep breath of car interior and press the automatic window control, so I can have the wind on my face. Real, rushing, moving, fresh air. It feels better than I could have ever imagined.

'You all right?' Dad asks.

'Yeah,' I say, and he can tell from the tone of my voice that I'm savouring every moment.

The town looks the same – no, it looks different. While I'd been in the unit I'd sometimes tried to remember places I'd known, but now I could see I hadn't got them quite right. They're hard and three-dimensional: a parade of shops with a video store, an off-licence, a hairdresser's offering half price for pensioners. We drive past an old pub that had been shut down for ages – now there's a half-built block of flats there. A big car showroom I knew wasn't there any more, its forecourt derelict. There are posters advertising a film I've never heard of, and completely new ads for McDonalds, for Orange, for Vodaphone. It's totally weird. The whole world has moved on. It's like I've been in prison or spent ages in another country; a hostage to my injury.

The sunshine, that black-and-white house with the wrought iron gates, the smell of petrol, the traffic lights turning to amber, the dog barking at the junction – everything fills me with a joy that almost brings tears to my eyes. I didn't think being on the outside would be this good. I'd forgotten that the world was so varied and colourful and noisy and interesting – I just can't take in the reality of it all.

Dad is going on about what Mum's arranged, and I'm pleased to see him looking happier. It's like old times – I'm coming home and the family is back together again, in every way.

My excitement rises as we get nearer to home. We turn into our street. I'm leaning forward, aching to see our house. And there it is. And we turn into the drive. And as we do, the front door opens and there's Mum, beaming from ear to ear.

Then I noticed they've put a ramp up over the front steps – that's for me. It jolts me. My house looks like an invalid's house. That's when I realise properly that it will be different – there's no going back – and I'll have to learn my house all over again, find out what I can and can't do, where I can and can't go. I know – because my dad's told me – that I'll be sleeping in the lounge; they've put a bed there, although that's only short-term. He's talking about getting an extension built, taking out a second mortgage.

Mum's opening the car door, kissing me, asking me about the journey; Dad's getting my chair out; and now I'm just hoping I'll be okay using the sliding board without any of the nurses being there. I have a moment of panic as I realise there are no nurses here, no staff, no one to sort me out if something goes wrong, except Mum and Dad. A district nurse is coming in the morning, but until then, we're on our own.

Dad's positioned the board, and now I'm moving with his help back into my chair, and Mum's getting me comfortable.

Then she takes control of my chair and pushes me up the ramp. Home. So familiar, so alien.

David comes out of the living room and says hi.

'Hi yourself,' I tell him.

He doesn't seem to know what to say. I notice now that he looks different. He's taller, ganglier, and comes over as awkward and embarrassed. I can tell he's growing up. I've become a stranger to him. I'll have to make a real effort to get to know him again. But any thoughts like that are blasted out of my head by Mum, who's asking me: do I want a drink or something to eat? Where would I like to go? Did I know Danny and Emma are coming over later? (I did.) And was I really sure I wanted to go to the pub tonight? (I was.)

Mum pushes me into the lounge and she and Dad get me onto the settee. Now I feel weird. I haven't sat on a settee since before the accident and I feel, as if for the first time, how much I've lost, how different I am. For a split-second I want to be back in the unit where I'm normal, not here where I'm a misfit. But the feeling passes and once again I just have an overpowering relief to be home.

I look around the living room, searching out familiar things. I see Dad's golfing trophies in the bookcase and . . . something's missing . . . I frown, trying to remember. My cups are missing. At the end of Year Eleven I was given a trophy for best sportsman – it had gone. I guess immediately that Mum has moved it, thinking it would make me feel bad to see it.

She comes in now with a coffee for me. She asks me where she should put it: would I like a table by me? Or would I like her to sit next to me and pass it to me, because it would be very hot and—

'Forget it,' I hear myself saying, not bothering to hide the irritation in my voice.

'I was only asking!' my mother says, and at her hurt I feel dreadful. I force myself to smile at her and apologise. But it's true – I know I've become bad-tempered; I'm easily made angry these days and I never used to be like that. Little things push me over the edge. Now I'm home, I know I must control myself. I tell Mum she should just put a table by me and I'll be fine. But I don't drink the coffee.

I look at my chair in the corner of the room and wish I was sitting there, where I can be mobile. At first I thought of my wheelchair as the badge of a cripple, but now I don't. It's an extension of me, it lets me go places. The other day, with Pete daring me, I'd gone up and down the kerb outside the unit – not just once, but twice, and then again. That was ace. I decide to ask Mum and Dad to get me back into my chair before Dan and Em arrive.

Mum's fluttering, nervous, as if I'm a complete stranger. Dad asks me if I want anything to eat, but she tells him off. She reminds him she's already asked me that! I can feel her pushing him away from me; see his look of momentary confusion. Again I feel a wave of anger. You'd have thought that on my homecoming, they'd make an effort to get on.

But no – that was plainly impossible. Part of me wants to sort their troubles out, as I used to. But also, now, part of me resents them.

Dad sits by me and begins to explain about the extension. 'It'll be more substantial than a conservatory,' he says. 'We'll need it plumbed too, as you'll have your own private bathroom, and you'll be virtually self-contained.'

A prisoner, I think, but just say, 'Great.' Then, 'It'll cost a packet.'

Dad smiles. 'We'll be getting help,' he says.

I pick up that he knows something that I don't, but I don't want to press him. I don't feel like talking about me. I'm actually a bit tired, drained after all the excitement. I'd just like to watch telly or something, but I feel if I say that they'll be upset. So I just sit there, a bit quiet. None of us quite knows what to do. Then David appears and asks if it's okay if he goes to the park to see his friends. The question's to Mum, but he glances at me. I grin at him to say that I understand and I don't mind.

Mum says, 'Okay, but be back for lunch.'

He mumbles something and goes. I ask Mum how he's been and she says, 'Fine – he's kept himself busy.' Mum tells me Dan will be round very soon and I ask to go back in my chair. She seems unsettled by that, but I'm helped back into it – and just in time, because I see Danny coming up the path. As Dad moves to open the door, I follow him.

Dan walks in as if nothing has changed, cool as you like.

I appreciate that. He says hi to my parents but cordially ignores them. He asks me how I'm doing in an ordinary, conversation-filler sort of way. I tell him we're in the lounge and he follows me. He takes a seat in the armchair nearest to where I park my chair. My parents are kind of hovering and I wish they'd go away.

Then I pick up Dan is a bit nervous about something. He's smiling a bit too much, he's glancing at my parents, and once more I get this sense that something's up.

Then he says, 'There's something I have to tell you.'

Don't ask me why, but immediately I think it's about Emma. She's not coming round – no, Dan's fallen for her and they're an item. The shock of it winds me.

'Go on,' I say.

'Well, have you heard of the Three Peaks Challenge?'

I'm a bit lost. I think for a moment and say, 'Isn't that when you climb Ben Nevis, Scafell and Snowdon in under twenty-four hours?'

Dan nods eagerly.

I may be a cripple but I'm not stupid. Everything suddenly makes sense. 'So you're doing it,' I accuse him. 'To raise money. To raise money for the unit?'

Dan shakes his head.

'To raise money for me?'

'You'll need a motor,' Dan says, matter-of-fact.

'And the extension,' my mum says at the same time.

Then Dan explains. He tells me the whole story: about

Mr Neale, about the kid in Year Seven, his training, the sponsorship. I don't know what to say. The whole thing's crazy, and I can't take on board that Dan would do all that for me. A horrible feeling of uselessness contends with a gratitude so powerful it robs me of words. But everyone's waiting for me to speak.

'I don't believe it,' I say.

Mum takes over, explains when it is, that she and Dad are going with them: Dad as driver, she as cook. Apparently they had only just found out too. And listening to them, I get used to the idea, but I have to admit I feel a bit jealous. I'd like to go too. And yet – to have my own car. I couldn't think of anything I'd like more. Not anything.

I'm feeling hungry now and so I tell Dan I'm going to see what's in the kitchen.

'No, it's all right,' says Mum. 'Just say what you want.'

I tense with irritation. 'Oh, whatever you've got.'

Dan glances at me, picks up the situation instantly. 'Tell you what,' he says. 'When Emma comes round, we'll go out. Take a walk around. Get some fresh air. All right?'

'Yeah!' I say. 'I'd really like that.'

DANNY

So there we were, the three of us, going down Elm Park Avenue: me, Simon on his wheels, and Emma on the other side. Sure, at first it felt weird, having Simon at such a low level, and it got me thinking about the way height matters. I look up to Mr Neale as he's so tall, but looking down on people is like a way of saying you don't respect them. But these were mixed-up thoughts. I found that after a while I got used to Simon being down there while we were up here. In fact, it was Si who broke the ice. 'I feel like I'm your kid and you two are playing Mum and Dad,' he says.

'It's because we're walking on either side of you,' Emma said quickly. She moved over to be next to me. Now I was in the middle. The plan was we'd go down to the park, cut through there and end up at the shops. I needed to get my dad a birthday card, Emma said she wanted some stuff, and Si fancied a magazine. Pretty boring, you'd think, but putting myself in Simon's position, I could see it spelt freedom. He looked good, determined, pushing the wheels of his chair with the palms of his hands like a pro.

I thought: this is how it's going to be now, and I realised it wasn't too bad. We were all together, all three of us, young, alive, with a future ahead of us, each one of us. I found myself humming a tune. I glanced at Em just as she glanced at me. We exchanged a smile and I cursed the feeling of weakness that swept through me. We turned into the park.

That was when it started.

As the three of us proceeded down the path that led to the lake, people looked. You'd see their eyes raking Simon, then staying for just a moment too long on him. You could see them thinking: what's wrong with him? Is he ill? A woman walked towards us with a child in tow; she flicked her eyes at Simon, then looked away deliberately. Her kid just stared. Then there was an old bloke and his wife who stood ceremoniously at the side of the path for us to go past, like a funeral procession.

I hoped Si hadn't noticed, but I was certain he had. I just kept up a conversation, gabbing on about anything I could think of. I found that every time people approached us, I steeled myself, waiting to see how they would react. It's true quite a few people just ignored us, but not everyone. Then some kid's ball hurtled from out of nowhere and came to rest just in front of us. I saw where the boys were who'd kicked it. I picked up the ball, passed it to Simon and he threw it back to them.

After a while he said to me, 'I need to conserve my energy. Will you push for a while?'

So I did, and more than ever found I came over all

protective. Emma took up position by Si and chatted to him. I was concentrating, looking out for pot-holes or anything that might jolt Simon or, worse still, tip him out. It was a responsibility, but one I was glad to get used to. Si could have had a power-assisted chair, but he didn't take to it. He said it made him feel like more of a cripple. So we passed the lake, caught a whiff of the rose garden, and came out through the park gates onto the road that led down to a junction, where the shops were.

We went into the newsagent's; I thought maybe I could get the card in there and Si could look at the magazines. Em stayed with him at the front of the shop, passing one or two down from the rack for him to look at. I went to the back where the cards were and, as I did, I noticed that even if I'd wanted Simon with me to help me choose, or read the ones with the filthy jokes and have a laugh, he couldn't have got through. The aisle was too narrow and there was a step or two to navigate.

I found a card with Homer Simpson on it and took it over to the till at the front. Em was already there with Simon. Si handed the mag up to the man at the till.

'That'll be two pound twenty,' the man said to Emma, ignoring Simon.

Si fumbled in his jacket pocket and handed the man a fiver. The bloke looked taken aback. He opened the till, took out some change, and then said to Simon, very slowly and loudly, 'That's two – pounds – eighty – change.'

'He's not deaf!' I snapped, but instantly regretted it. Everyone froze with embarrassment. We left the shop as quickly as we could. Emma shoved the mag down the side of Simon's chair. 'Cretin,' I muttered. Simon just laughed.

There was also a small supermarket at the junction, and we went in there as Emma needed a few things. Now I found I was on the alert for people's reactions, primed to notice the slightest deviation in their response to Simon. So naturally I noticed when, at the checkout, the woman in the Lo-Cost overall cast Simon pitying glances and then couldn't resist engaging him in conversation, ignoring the rest of us.

'Nice day to get out and about,' she said.

'Yeah, it is,' Simon replied.

'Because you need a bit of fresh air; we all do. Have you got everything you want? Do you need any help with the packing?'

'No, it's okay.'

'Of course. I can see you've got your friends with you. That's nice, love. It's nice to have good friends. But if there's anything we can help you with, just say, pet.'

I cringed.

Later on we went into McDonald's, where there were no steps and a table where Si could park his chair. Emma joined the queue to get us all some fries.

'It pisses me off,' I said to Si, 'the way people treat you. Like you're some kind of alien.'

'They warned me about that at the unit.'

'Don't you feel angry?' I said, seething with anger myself.

'No – there's no point. You've got to shrug it off, learn to live with it.'

'I don't agree,' I told him. 'I don't see why able-bodied people should get away with staring at you like you're a sideshow. Or treating you like some charity case. It's like a sort of racism – they're, like . . . disablists. Disablist bastards!'

'I know, but not everyone's uncomfortable with disability, just like not everyone's racist. And the ones that are – well, they're just ignorant.'

'Yeah, but that's the kind of ignorance that leads to people leaving their cars in disabled parking spots, or using words like "spazz".'

Simon just smiled at me. He evidently didn't want to talk about it any more. But I'd only just got going. Emma came back with our fries.

'But everyone was making prejudiced assumptions about you – like you're ill, or stupid or something!' I carried on.

'I know,' Emma said, 'but if Si is angry about that all the time, he'll just get a chip on his shoulder.'

Time to defuse the situation. I took one of the fries and placed it on his shoulder. We all laughed as it tumbled down. Si lobbed a handful of his fries at me. I threw some back. Now we were really attracting everyone's attention.

'Anyway,' Emma continued, when Si and I had stopped our mock-fight with the fries, 'when people see Si, they just think he's broken his leg or something, because he's young and looks okay.'

'Just okay?' Simon teased her.

'No, gorgeous,' she said, and leant over to kiss him. She flushed as she did so. I turned my head away.

SIMON

'Are you sure you're going to be warm enough?' Mum says. 'And get Dan to ring if you need to come back early for any reason.'

'I'll be fine,' I tell her.

'Let me just pull down your jeans leg – there, that's better!'

Stop it! I scream inside. My mum's fussing is driving me mad. I can't wait for Dan to get here and help my dad get me into the car. More than anything I want to be in the Coach and Horses, away from all this suffocating attention. Honestly, I prefer the way my younger bro just ignores me.

I try to dispel my bad temper. It's funny, Danny was getting all worked up about that shopkeeper and the woman at the checkout, but that kind of thing doesn't bother me too much. It's more when the people I know get in the way of my independence. I have to live with the way I am now and I don't want to be beholden to anyone. I know that to some extent I will be, I accept that. But I want to do things for myself, I can't have this continual fussing. I take a few deep breaths to calm myself. I'm nervous – nervous at the prospect of a night in the boozer? I must be mad as well as crippled!

Dan's here, and there's all that business with the sliding board again, and then we're off. Dad explains he's only too happy to pick us up and to give him a ring whenever we're ready. Dan tells me everyone's going to be there and again I get this weird feeling of excitement mixed with apprehension.

I push myself into the pub. It's pretty busy, but one advantage of being a cripple is that people make way for you. Then I hear a scream: 'Simon!' – it's Jen, and I see her at a back table. I can't help smiling now and I make my way towards her.

She's out of her seat and all over me, big sloppy kisses, and squeezes. She smells good – some rich, musky perfume, so different to the hospital. 'Omigod!' she squeals. 'You look – kind of older, and more muscly!' I flex my biceps. She prods them. 'Rock hard!' she says.

Steph comes over and kisses me too, a light feather of a kiss, her lips like the flick of a butterfly's wings on my cheek. I've noticed this thing – since the accident the rest of my body is more sensitive than ever, as if my skin is compensating for the loss of sensation elsewhere.

I like the girls kissing me, then feel guilty as I realise Emma is there too, holding back, letting the others make a fuss. She's sitting quietly, a glass of wine in front of her. 'Hi,' I say.

Dan brings the drink over, just as Wilko and Adam arrive. Everyone's high-spirited, celebratory, and I love it, I feel like I'm having a life again. I breathe in all the pub smells – tobacco, beer, the whiff of disinfectant from the Gents, the floral polish on the table; it's great to be here. This is the best I've felt for ages. We're all sitting round a table and I'm just Simon again, Simon with my mates.

Wilko's stressing about his exams, says he can't work. We carry on drinking beer. The girls give him a lecture. Danny and Adam are remembering a programme late last night on TV, some new comedy. I saw it too and we have a laugh about it. I'm normal again, and find I'm drinking quickly. I can feel the alcohol affecting me, making me talkative, excited.

I turn to Danny and say to him, 'Thanks.'

'For what?' he asks.

'For sticking around,' I say. 'And also for the Three Peaks thing.'

Danny grins at me. 'I thought you might be mad. I should have told you earlier.'

'It's okay,' I say, and then I think of everything Dan has done for me: the visits, the jokes, the way he's kept me connected to everyone, and now he's facing this challenge to get me more independence, and – I think it's partly the booze – I feel my eyes stinging and my chest swelling. I'm shocked as I realise I'm close to tears.

I take a big, deep breath. Then there's a welcome distraction. All the girls get up on one of their expeditions to the Ladies. We all make way for them. It's quiet once they go. I look round the pub, just people-watching. Then a girl catches my eye – she's good-looking, short dark hair, large eyes. She smiles. Do I know her from somewhere? I look away, then look back. This time she smiles at me. No, I don't think I do know her. But, hey, I smile back. I see she's with a couple of other girls. They start whispering and the dark-haired girl gives me another smile. I feel myself getting nervous, but nicely so.

I turn to tune in to what Dan and Adam are saying. Next thing, the girl's moved over, her friends by her side. 'Hi!' she says to me.

Her friend, who's slightly drunk, says to Dan, 'My mate, Rochelle, fancies your mate.'

I'm taken aback. I realise she hasn't noticed I'm in a wheelchair. I feel panicky and steel myself for the moment she finds out.

'He's spoken for,' says Danny. 'But *I'm* not.'

Then I interrupt. I don't know why I say this and hate myself as I do. 'I'm a cripple,' I tell her. And indicate my chair.

She doesn't react at all. 'So what?' she says, still giving me the eye. Then she crouches down. '*Do* you have a girlfriend?' she asks. That obviously bothers her more.

'Yes,' Danny says for me.

She gets up. 'Better luck next time.' She grins and walks off.

Dan laughs. 'You're still a babe magnet,' he says.

What I remember is the way she saw my chair and didn't care. I could see it in her face – she didn't give a toss. She was a girl on the pull and that was all that mattered.

Before I have time to properly consider this, Em, Steph and Jen are back from the Ladies, and they make themselves comfortable again. Emma comes to sit next to me. I take her hand and squeeze it. I'm glad she's mine. That girl, the one with the short dark hair, has made me feel okay again. I realise Emma might not have stopped fancying me and maybe I haven't stopped fancying her. In some strange way I've taken Em for granted, and I mustn't do that.

I kiss her hard, and don't mind that everyone's there and watching.

EMMA

Dan was watching and so were Steph and Jen. I didn't kiss Simon back, I just waited until he'd finished – because it didn't feel like he was kissing me for *me*, but kissing me to show he owned me. When it was over, I tried to smile and glanced at Dan, who had his face turned away from me, saying something funny to Wilko.

I wanted to cry all over again. This mess I'd got myself into was getting worse by the hour, and I didn't know what to do about it. Nor did Jen and Steph.

When we'd arrived in the Ladies, Jen had said to me, 'What's up?'

'What do you mean?' I retorted, getting my brush out of my bag and brushing my hair vigorously.

'You've been dead quiet. She has, hasn't she, Steph?'

Steph nodded. My friends were standing behind me, reflected in the mirror.

Steph said, 'It's to do with Simon, isn't it? Something's wrong.'

I didn't respond, just carried on brushing.

'We've been worried about you,' Steph said. 'Something's up, isn't it?'

I wanted to tell them everything, but how could I? What would they think of me, knowing that all I did, every day and every night, was dream of Danny, replaying all the conversations we'd had, looking at old photos of him, crying myself to sleep, sometimes? I was ashamed of myself. Maybe I could have told them about my feelings for Danny when they started, but not now, not when they'd got so out of hand.

'Emma?' Steph gently persisted.

I was crying, I could feel tears trickling down my face. I couldn't tell them – they would hate me.

Jen hugged me tight. 'We're your mates,' she said. 'We'll understand.'

Now I was crying properly and it was a relief. Just crying wasn't giving anything away. I could allow myself this luxury.

Steph said, 'I think I know what's going on. You're worried Simon's feelings have changed, that he's ignoring you. But he's just so excited to be back with us all.'

I was able to control my tears now – I had to, otherwise the lads would know I'd been sobbing my heart out. I shook my head, to tell Steph she wasn't right.

'It's just me,' I explained. 'It's stress, probably. Exam nerves.'

Jen teased. 'Or something totally bizarre, like she's fallen for Danny!'

I froze. Had they realised? Should I joke that I had fallen

for him, or deny it, or even admit it? I quickly tried to cover my confusion.

'Danny? Don't make me laugh.'

Jen and Steph exchanged a glance. Steph, everybody's agony aunt, took over.

'You *have* fallen for him! Omigod! But I can see exactly what's happened. You've spent so much time with him in the last few months. And he's changed so much, he's fitter and stopped all that messing around. It's almost like he's *become* Simon. And Simon's changed too – I don't mean because of his injury, but in his character. It's like he's got this tough shell around him now – and he needs it, every bit of it – but he isn't the same boy you fell in love with last year. He isn't, is he, Em?'

Her words died away. Jen hugged me again and said, 'It's okay.' I cried a little more. She asked me, 'Does Dan know?'

'No,' I said. 'Not at all. And he'd never, ever think of me in that way because of Simon.'

I told them everything, then. About the time when Simon tried to finish with me and I refused. How I just wished I could be his best mate. How, very, very secretly, I had to admit his injury *did* make a difference to me. I loved him, I felt sorry for him, but I didn't fancy him – only I wanted to do the right thing. I sacrificed my true feelings so I could be there for Simon, and knew I would have to sacrifice my feelings for Danny too.

My friends were brilliant. They told me not to feel guilty,

that I'd done the best I could. That any time I wanted to talk, they'd listen. That maybe I ought to think about having a talk with Simon? But I said no, it would sound as if I was dumping him and I wasn't prepared to do that.

Bit by bit I calmed down. We decided that now wasn't the time to deal with this situation, that it was Simon's first night in the pub, and we'd go back and join the others as if nothing had happened. I could do that, because the relief I felt in having told Jen and Steph was huge, vaster than the ocean.

So we came back, and Simon kissed me. And I found I couldn't respond to his kiss at all, and that back there, in the talk I'd just had with the girls, something had changed for ever. Having admitted how I felt, I knew I was a fraud, being there with Simon. In some way I'd betrayed him. So I tried harder than ever to be jolly, to be affectionate. I played with his hair a bit, laughed loudly at Wilko's jokes, even though they were getting more rubbish by the minute. But inside I felt hollow and confused.

And, every so often, I saw Dan looking at me. Maybe it was my imagination, because I was so sensitive to everything he did. Maybe he was feeling critical of me, thinking I'd had too much to drink. The pub was hot and noisy and I was beginning to wish I was somewhere else. My crying fit had left me feeling weak and drained.

Then Simon said, 'If you lot don't mind, I think I'll call it a day.'

He finished his beer, and everyone agreed it was probably time to go. I tried not to sound too eager.

'I'll ring my dad,' Simon announced. 'He's picking me up.'

He fumbled in his pocket for his phone. I could tell he was finding it hard to get a grip on it. 'Here,' I said. 'Let me.' I reached into his pocket and passed it to him.

'Shove off,' he snapped at me. 'I'm not that helpless.'

It was partly his words, but mostly the tone of his voice – vicious, unwarranted, downright mean. The shock robbed me of the power to answer back. Simon had never spoken to me like that before. Everyone had noticed. I was embarrassed, and scared I was going to cry again in front of everyone. So I got up and said, 'Excuse me,' and left the pub.

In a moment I was outside in the street. I didn't know what to do. I just wanted to get as far away as possible from the whole mess and my boyfriend, who'd become a stranger to me. I thought the best thing to do would be to go home. So I started walking towards the junction, where the bus stop was.

I walked quickly, not able yet to think through everything that had happened. At the back of my mind I thought I shouldn't be out alone so late at night, as the Coach and Horses wasn't in the best area. But to be honest, I didn't care. I felt as if I didn't mind what happened to me now. I'd made a mess of everything. I was so churned up inside that it was a few moments before I registered the sound of footsteps, getting faster and faster. Someone was after me.

So, instinctively, I started running, glancing over my shoulder to see who was chasing me. It was Dan.

'Emma!'

Within a moment he was by my side. He grabbed me and swung me round to face him.

'Are you okay?'

It was the relief he wasn't a stranger, it was my hurt at Simon's words, it was . . . it was because he was Dan. I buried myself in him and sobbed.

In a moment he was covering my face with kisses, murmuring my name. I thought I was dreaming. I lifted my face fully to his and our mouths met.

It was almost as if everyone else had ceased to exist, only Danny and I mattered. I wanted to get as close to him as I could. It was like this moment was all we had, and there was never going to be enough time to express how we felt. I was crying – no, someone else was crying: it was him. Danny was crying too. He pulled me tight towards him and there was only this one thing in the whole, entire universe – us.

And then it was over. A car drove slowly past, illuminating us in its headlights.

'You shouldn't have left Simon,' I said.

'He's all right. Adam will stay with him.'

'I shouldn't have run out like that,' I said.

'You were shocked,' Danny said, his fingers in my hair. 'But you mustn't take it personally. He's like that now. He shouts at me sometimes too. And it's more stressful than you think for him, going home for the first time.' He kissed me again. I kissed him back. 'I think Simon finds his parents difficult. He feels smothered by them.'

'Yes,' I said, running my hands down Dan's lean body. 'And then he's got to transfer back to the unit tomorrow and it's as if he's taking a step backwards.'

Dan kissed the top of my head. I thought: we're not talking about what's happening to us here. But I was too scared to start.

He said, 'Shall I take you home?'

I said, 'It's all right. I can get the bus.'

'I'll come with you,' he insisted.

Entwined together, we caught the bus. We went upstairs, as far away from the other passengers as possible. I thought to myself: if we only ever have this night, it will be enough. I wanted it to last for ever.

The bus lurched towards my street. We spoke about Simon, about the others, never about ourselves – not until we'd arrived at my street, got off the bus, and were standing outside my front door.

Then Danny said, 'I don't know what to do, Emma.'

I whispered, 'Neither do I.'

A light went on in the hall. I knew it was my mum. She opened the door and Dan broke away.

'I'll call you,' he said.

In a moment he was gone, and my mum was asking how the evening had gone. How was Simon? Did he enjoy himself? I answered her questions briefly and said I was tired, I needed to go to bed.

'Who was that with you?' she asked.

'Dan. He saw me home.'

'I like Dan,' Mum said. 'He's a nice boy.'

I was already halfway up the stairs. I entered my bedroom and shut the door. Slowly I lowered myself onto the bed and sat there, stunned. I took a deep breath, wanting to smell Danny again, to remember the feel and taste of his kisses, the push of his body against mine. But all I could feel was his absence.

A voice in my head said, *you've betrayed Simon. You cheated on him. With his best friend.*

But it wasn't like that. I couldn't help it.

You could.

I made fists of my hands and dug my fingernails into my palms to control the surge of anguish that was overpowering me. I wasn't going to let myself suffer. Now, I only wanted to think about Dan.

Did all of that really happen? Had I dreamed it? To reassure myself, I tried to remember it all, from when Dan found me on the street, to how he started kissing me, to him telling me that he cares about me . . .

He'd said he'd call. I got my phone out of my pocket, laid it carefully on my bed, and willed it to ring.

But what would Dan say? I just didn't know where we could go from here. If only time could stop. If only we could just live in tonight for the rest of our lives. But already I could hear my mum getting ready for bed, saw my alarm clock change its digits, knew I'd also have to go to bed, and wake up tomorrow and face it all.

I'd just got back from the bathroom when my phone announced a text. I checked who it was from. Dan. I swallowed hard and read what he had to say.

DANNY

Forget it ever happened.

No, I couldn't send that – it was too brutal. And I would never forget this night. I cleared the words from the screen and started again.

It shouldn't have happened. Let's still be friends.

But that made it sound as if I was just led by my libido – and it was a lot more than that. And I knew I was still lying. I deleted it.

I love you, Emma.

My finger hovered above the 'send' key. The slightest pressure, and there would be no going back. The one thing I had learnt tonight was that Emma cared about me too. But how would Simon deal with that? One by one, I cleared the letters off the screen of my phone.

How could I find some words that were kind to her, kind to Simon, and didn't lie?

You know how I feel. It's up to you.

Then I added: **And Simon.**

And pressed 'send'.

EMMA

It's up to me. And Simon. Dan was right, but I put off what I knew I had to do. My excuse was exams. It was AS Levels, and I thought: best not to do anything drastic now, for Dan's sake, for my sake, but most of all, for Simon's sake. He was in his last few weeks at the unit – what a time for me to dump him!

So Dan and I avoided each other. Only once, as he brushed past me in the English corridor, did he stroke my hand briefly – and his touch was like electricity. For the rest of the time we said nothing. No one in school would have ever guessed what there was between us, which was just as well. In fact, Danny was busy with last minute preparations for the Three Peaks Challenge as well as revision, so it was easy not to see too much of him.

I carried on visiting Simon, and we remained the best of friends. Of course he'd apologised for shouting at me, and guiltily I told him I'd forgiven him immediately. I said sorry for running off. He commented that it was good of Dan to look after me. I agreed. There was a moment of awkwardness – or maybe I imagined that. And afterwards, we were never alone that much, and when we were, we just talked *at* each other: I told him how nervous I was about the exams; he told me about the last stages of his rehab, how he was using a standing frame now and how he was top of the league in the unit's pool tournament.

Simon was more and more active; meanwhile, I tried sitting in the garden and revising, but my thoughts always drifted off to Danny, replaying that night at the Coach and Horses, trying to remember every single detail. Only the more I did that, the more I felt as if I'd made it all up. Gently, I pulled myself back to the notes I had to learn.

And my life remained like that – wistful, yearning, unresolved – until the last exam, English. For three hours I'd written helter-skelter, pouring out everything I knew about the books, praying it was relevant, knowing I wasn't expressing myself very well but not caring, just hoping luck was with me. When I finally finished, I looked up at the clock and saw I had fifteen minutes left.

With the words of my English teacher ringing in my ears, I began to read through what I had written. I didn't like doing that – my own essays always sound stupid to me, and I was too tired to think of any way of improving them. So, with ten minutes to go, I replaced the top on my pen and looked around the sports hall where the exams were held. The floor was covered with protective sheeting, which had a distinctive rubbery smell. I could hear the occasional rustling of paper, saw a teacher patrolling the aisles out of the corner of my eye. Some people around me had finished too; others were still scribbling away. The atmosphere was peaceful and intense at the same time.

I felt an overwhelming relief that the exams were finished. It washed over me like a wave, then receded to leave something clear and sparkling in its wake. Which was this: I decided to go to the unit that night and tell Simon everything. That basically my feelings for him had changed. That I'd become involved with Dan. And he could shout and rave and tell me he would never speak to me again. I would endure it.

I know this seems brutal. But was there ever going to be a good time to tell him the truth? He was coming home for good on Monday – the day after the weekend of Dan's Three Peaks Challenge. So did I tell him then, or the next week, while he's getting used to life at home? I realised, as the invigilator passed and re-passed me, that not telling Simon was a kind of lie, a lie by omission. To let our dead relationship drag on was an act of cruelty to him, kind only to me. For the past was dead and nothing could resurrect it now. Our relationship died for good the day Danny kissed me and I kissed him back.

The teacher announced that there was five minutes to go. I looked over to where Dan was sorting through his script. My heart seized with love for him. I had a sudden fear that he'd gone off me, or thought better of it – but then I realised those were the scared thoughts of a child. The fact was that Dan and I had *grown* to care for each other, and it was

Simon who had done it, Simon who had brought us together – all without his knowledge. I recognised then that it was up to me to explain all that to him.

Once everyone had got out of the exam hall, compared answers and made plans for a night out, I got away from school. As I walked towards the bus station I texted my mother to tell her I'd be home late – in the last few moments I had made up my mind I wanted to speak to Simon as soon as possible.

I had to take two buses to get to the hospital. On the first bus, I noticed Simon's brother David. He was larking around with some of the boys in his year. They were at the front, mock-fighting, shouting, and swearing. I was a bit taken aback – David never used to be like that. I felt a little anxious: was he all right? I used to be quite close to David. He'd taught me games on his PlayStation, and told me about his new class when he transferred to our school. He and his friends got off the bus before me and, as they swaggered through, David caught my eye. I called to him that I was going to the unit. He blushed; one of his mates wolf-whistled and whispered to David, something about me, I guessed. He stumbled as he got off the bus.

But I was too preoccupied with my forthcoming ordeal to think much about him. I was wondering why, on the two opportunities I'd had to break with Simon – when the nurse spoke to me, and when Simon himself tried to end it – I had refused. The first time, perhaps, I wasn't ready; the second,

I realised my pity for him had made me dishonest. It occurred to me that *not* to tell him how I really felt was insulting to him; it was treating him first and foremost as a victim. He would hate that. Simon might be a wheelchair-user, but he was a whole person, strong enough to deal with the cards life dealt to him. And some of those cards were pretty rotten. Including an unfaithful girlfriend.

I reached the unit and walked swiftly through the hospital grounds. As I came into the lobby I glanced into the common room, where Simon was chatting with Tiny Tim. I entered and said hi. Simon looked happy, wheeled himself over to me, and explained that a guy from some organisation had been giving a talk and as a result he was going to try for a wheelchair rugby team. He was explaining how the local team plays regular tournaments and there could even be a chance to compete in the Paralympics. He was full of what he'd just heard and talked without a pause.

After a while he noticed I was quiet. 'What's wrong?' he asked.

'Nothing,' I lied.

'Let's go out for a bit,' he said. We were so close, I felt he knew what I was thinking. That was the worst part – those few minutes before we began talking.

Together we left the unit and made our way to a small garden where there was a bench or two. It was a place where some of the in-patients and the nurses had a quick smoke and others took some fresh air. I sat on one of the benches, opposite a couple of shrubs. Simon parked himself at an angle to me, so we could see each other. 'Did the exam go badly?' he asked.

I shook my head. I wished I could find the right words to say this. I realised, despite all the scenarios I'd played in my head, that I hadn't a clue how to begin. Do I finish with him first, or tell him about Danny first? I felt sick with nerves, hating myself for what I was about to do.

'I just think . . .' My voice sounded tiny and pathetic. 'I just think, we need to talk . . .'

SIMON

'. . . about our relationship.'

I swallow hard. I've been waiting for this day. From the time I woke up after my accident and began to put together the shattered pieces of my life, I've known this was going to happen. My heart starts pounding at the same time as a heaviness almost robs me of the power to speak.

'I think I know what you're going to say,' I tell Emma, and I take her hand. Her hand is limp in mine.

I take a few deep breaths. I brace myself. A tear rolls down Emma's cheek. I remove my hand from hers to brush it away.

'It's okay,' I reassure her. 'It's okay.'

'I love you as much as ever,' she protests, 'but just not . . .'

'In that way,' I finish for her.

She nods, dumbly. A crashing misery hits me and sends me reeling. But I try not to show it.

'I thought so,' I say.

We're quiet for a bit. I try to process this. A couple of months ago, I would have been glad. I know I tried to finish with her myself but, since she refused, I'd started to depend on her. What would I do without Emma now? I panic, grip the sides of my chair.

'Please can we still be friends?' she begs me.

'Of course, Em.'

'I'm sorry.'

'Me too,' I say, but not cruelly. The better part of me knows this is tough for her, and if I give her a hard time, I'll regret it. My mind works quickly. I think that perhaps it's better this way – better that I start entirely afresh when I go home. Maybe I've been clinging to Emma. Maybe it's only a break we need. I could handle that. I might even enjoy the freedom. I manage a smile. She smiles at me through her tears.

'This is so hard,' she says, 'because I still care about you.'

'But you're being honest,' I tell her, 'and I appreciate that.'

She sniffs and reaches for a tissue. Now I test my feelings; I tell myself again – Emma's just dumped me. But there's just a numbness, no real misery. There's even the beginning of relief. I think: now I'm only responsible for myself, no one else. I can see that the last eight months have been hard for Emma too. I begin to realise this really is for the best. I find I'm feeling better very quickly.

I speak again. I say: 'I'm glad you had the guts to tell me this – I think you've done the right thing for both of us.'

She smiles, a lovely, radiant smile.

Life without Emma . . . No, I won't be without her. She'll be as much my friend as Danny is – she'll be my mate.

'You'll be my mate.' I utter my thoughts aloud.

She nods vigorously. 'More than ever, Si. More than ever. Don't think you'll ever get rid of me.'

'I'm counting on that,' I tease her. Then I continue. 'And just to show there's no hard feelings, I'm going to let you in on a secret. Tiny Tim's arranged for him and his sister to drive me to the bottom of Snowdon, to be there when Dan finishes the Three Peaks.'

'That's brilliant! He'll so love that!'

'Would you like to come too?' I ask her.

I see an odd look on her face. There's hesitation there, even embarrassment. For a moment I think maybe she's planned something for the end of the Challenge and I've spoilt it. I'm puzzled.

Then she says, 'Yes. Okay. Let's do that. What shall I do? Meet you here, or what?'

I see a muscle jump in her cheek. I put her nervousness down to the fact she's just dumped me.

'Dan reckons they'll finish around half four or five. So we're setting off at nine to give us plenty of time, to allow for stops and that. Can you be here for nine?'

'Yes. Yes, I can.'

Emma smiles again, a sweet, sad smile. I know how she feels. Breaking up is painful, but as we speak I realise more and more that this is the best thing that could have happened. We'd become best friends rather than boyfriend/girlfriend. Maybe it was inevitable. I'm far less upset than I expected to be. And also – to be completely honest – every so often I'm distracted; thinking about what the man from the Wheelchair Rugby Association has been telling us. Okay, so wheelchair rugby's more like basketball than rugby, but full chair contact is allowed and the game's fast and exciting. And next week I'm going to see the Eagles play against the Bandits. Flashes of excitement mix in with my regret about Emma. Maybe she feels this more badly than I do. Sometimes it's harder to dump than to be dumped.

We talk a little more. Emma's understandably quiet and thoughtful. When she leaves to go, she appears almost defeated and, perversely, I'm glad it hurts her so much to part from me. She kisses me and leaves.

I stay outside a little longer, enjoying the sensation of the sun on my skin. It's strange, but I don't mind that we've split. The relationship has run its course. It's not as if she's fallen for anyone else. That would be tough. Who knows, maybe we'd have broken up even *without* my injury.

I sit there feeling clean and clear, as if I'm entering into a new phase of my life. I want to be alone to make the most of it and I like the feeling of having no ties, no responsibilities. On a good day – and today *is* a good day, despite Emma's bombshell – I can see that even with my injury I can have a full life with sport, study, friends and even girlfriends. On bad days I mourn for my past life, but only as you do for something that's prematurely dead. I know I can never have it back.

There's one more thing I have to do, however, and Emma has given me the guts to do it. So later that afternoon when Mum arrives, while I'm still feeling my way around this new space that's my freedom, I tell her, also, that we need to talk. She seems quite cheerful – the Three Peaks Challenge has been preoccupying her too. We go over to my bed and I'm glad to notice that the ward is empty. She sits on my bed and asks me what I want.

'It's about when I come home.'

'Fire away.'

'I don't want you and Dad to bother with an extension.'

She frowns, puzzled. 'But you can have a self-contained flat of your own! We won't bother you. It's an ideal solution.'

'It'll be a waste of money. Because, once I've finished at school, I'll be wanting to go away to uni.'

She's silent now, absorbing this. 'But you can go to a local university.'

'I want to go *away*. I won't want to live at home for ever.'

'But who will look after you?'

'I will. *I'll* look after me.'

'You won't be able to manage by yourself. What if you get ill? You heard what the nurse said about sudden rises in blood pressure – what if it sets in, you get dizzy and no one's around? What if you fall?' Her voice rises with anxiety. Her concern reaches out like tentacles and entwines me.

'I'll work out a system. A lot of the guys who've been in the unit have flats of their own. They manage.'

'Yes, but they don't have families. They don't have mothers.' She was advancing like an army; she was raising the stakes; she was making me attack her.

'I'm seventeen now and I'm growing up. In the normal order of things, I would have left home anyway in a year.'

'It's different now.'

'No, it isn't.'

'Simon, I thought you'd come a long way in accepting what's happened to you. We've all said how well you've coped. But acceptance means accepting your limitations. You'll need me.'

I say, 'Don't you think maybe *you* need *me?*'

Like a bomb, my words explode and mushroom, obscuring the space between us. I wish I hadn't said that. But I'd thought it, often. Being away from home had made me see how Mum had clung to me ever since that business with Dad, how I'd become a kind of substitute partner. And for Mum, my paralysis made that more true than ever; in her mind, I would always be there with her.

I glance at Mum and I can't tell what she's thinking. Something tightens and hardens in her face. I see her picking up the mantle of righteousness – that expression parents have when they know they're old and right, while you are young and stupid and don't know what's good for you.

'Simon, this isn't about my needs and wants – it's about you. We're working out what's best for *you*.'

'You can't stop me,' I say, realising instantly how young I'm sounding, and how I'm playing into her hands.

'I wouldn't *stop* you,' she sighs.

I shift ground now. 'I'll have a talk with Dad. See what he thinks.'

She flashes a look at me, then lowers her eyes. 'He won't interfere. He's washed his hands of everything to do with you and your injury. He can't cope.'

I think to myself, that's not entirely true. I wonder how much Mum needs the fiction of him not being able to cope, so that *she* can cope. But I decide to say nothing. I'm not liking this conversation. When Emma dumped me, I felt secretly relieved; I'd imagined that when I told Mum I wanted to leave home, she'd feel relieved too. Only she's twisting it and she's making me feel guilty.

'Let's drop it, Mum,' I say.

I wonder whether she thinks she's won, that I'll reconsider and contemplate a life at home. But the prospect seems like a sort of living death. I know some SCIs live with their parents as long as they can, but it seems to me they're the sort of people who would have stayed at home anyway. I'd always imagined a life of my own, travelling, maybe working in medicine – there's no way I'm giving that vision up, injury or no injury.

'This is all part of the trauma of going home,' Mum says. 'Let's forget we had this conversation. It's good that you can stay in the unit during the Three Peaks. David's arranged to sleep over with a friend – Tony Melton – for the weekend. Do you know him?'

'No.'

She reaches across and ruffles my hair. 'I know how you feel, Simon. But, really, home is the best place for you. You'll see that.'

Will I? I wonder.

DANNY

I found myself getting impatient. There were so many preliminaries – packing the Galaxy with the food, the primus stove, Robert going through the checklist: 'Waterproofs – check! Torch – check! Whistle – check! Bivvy bag – check!' Did he *really* think we'd have to bivouac on a mountain top and sleep in that thing? Meanwhile John was fiddling with the maps. It seemed an age before we eased out of Robert's drive, with Juliet and the kids waving us off.

When you actually measure the amount of walking we had to do, it doesn't sound much. Twenty-two miles – kids' stuff. But we were going to have to climb nearly ten thousand feet and drive five hundred miles – all in under twenty-four hours. Robert and Calvin had worked on timings, and we were reasonably confident. We'd climb Ben Nevis in the evening, then Scafell at the crack of dawn, which would give us plenty of time to head south and then west to reach Snowdon by lunchtime.

Robert and Calvin were in high spirits. Calvin was running through his sponsors and Robert was explaining about glaciation. John and Sylvia were in the front, not speaking, but listening to some boring old play on the radio.

I stared out of the window at the traffic, read the sides of the lorries we passed: Eddie Stobart, Tesco's, Norbert Dentressangle.

Emma had called round last night, to wish me luck. When I opened the door to her, I tried to read her face and I could see immediately that she looked unhappy. I didn't know what that meant. We went into the garden, as the rest of my family were watching TV. I could feel that she had something to tell me and my nervousness made me clumsy. I bumped into her as we wandered through the garden. We came to rest by the rose bush. We stood close, but not touching. She looked down.

She told me that she'd seen Simon yesterday and finished with him. I caught my breath. I was torn between pity for Simon and happiness for me. Anyway, I said nothing. I could feel my heart pounding in my chest.

'But I didn't tell him about us,' she said. 'I couldn't.'

There was a moment of confusion as I tried to take that in. Was she saying that she'd changed her mind about her feelings for me? No – I quickly guessed what had happened. She simply couldn't tell Simon that she'd got involved with me – it would be the final kick in the teeth, the worst kind of betrayal. Her courage had failed her – mine would have failed me too.

'It was bad enough . . .' she explained, hesitantly, 'it was bad enough just ending it.'

'Yeah,' I agreed.

It was so hard to be that close to her in the garden. I wanted to hug her and hold on to her. Instead I found a rose that was past its best and tore off its petals one by one. She watched me, mesmerised.

Then I asked, 'What we will do now?'

'I don't know,' Emma replied, and the distress in her voice almost pleased me. We were both hurting. The roses gave off a heavy scent.

Cruising along the motorway now, I could almost taste the scent of those roses, just as I could feel the pain of being so close to Emma, with nothing resolved. But try as I could, I couldn't remember her face. I wanted to visualise it, but it had gone. I just saw parts of her in my mind's eye – the way her hair fell, the flash of her eyes, the curve of her hips.

She didn't stay long. We talked about the Challenge and she said she was meeting the girls in town. When she left, we didn't touch, we avoided each other. Mum shouted that it was good of Emma to call, and I said, yeah, it was, and went up to my room, and threw myself on my bed. I could have yelled with frustration.

But then common sense took over. Tomorrow was the Challenge. I had to be fit. I couldn't afford to be getting into an emotional state. How pathetic *was* I? I decided I wasn't going to let thoughts of Emma get in the way of the Three Peaks. I had to cut off. I had to focus.

Already I'd broken my resolution, sitting here, thinking of Emma. So I brought my mind back to the task in hand.

I was wearing shorts and a T-shirt, but round my waist I'd tied the rugby shirt Simon had given me on my seventeenth birthday. It was my mascot – it was something of him I was taking with me.

We drove through Fort William and came to Glen Nevis ahead of schedule. Robert suggested we eat, and set off around four. I didn't see why we couldn't go right away. The mountain reared up in front of us and I could see the path stretching out, and I wanted to be on it, moving. The Visitor Centre was busy, and that was the first time it occurred to me we wouldn't be alone; there were a number of teams attempting the Challenge. Robert was busy introducing himself to virtually all of them.

After a late lunch Calvin and I just kicked a ball around. It was a warm afternoon, with only the merest hint of a breeze. The sky was blue, just flecked with white clouds. I'd said to Robert we'd have a spectacular view. He said not to count on it. Ben Nevis could pull a few surprises.

Finally the time came for us to start. I eased my feet into my boots and laced them tight; I checked through my rucksack and hoisted it onto my shoulders. Robert looked at his watch – half past four – and that was it, we were off. Nothing to it.

We walked together at a fair pace up the path that led to the summit. We passed lots of other walkers. Somehow I'd imagined Ben Nevis as imposing, forbidding, yet these lower slopes were nothing out of the ordinary, not much different to Ash Edge. I was getting uncomfortably warm and looked forward to getting to where the air was cooler. I could feel my legs losing their stiffness and accustoming themselves to the hike up. I was feeling optimistic, capable, confident we'd do it.

'This is the boring bit,' Calvin chirped by my side. 'It's just a long haul, but it'll get steeper soon. I was checking out the gradients and . . .'

I didn't listen. I was getting into a rhythm now, enjoying the sense of pushing myself and getting higher. The slopes of the mountain lay on either side of me, rising sheer, bare rock, with just tussocks of grass near the path. I liked the sense of the ascent and the compulsion to go up, get higher, reach the top. The drop on either side of me gave me an adrenaline rush – it was the remnant of my fear of heights. We strung out along the path: me in front, Calvin just behind me, and Robert bringing up the rear.

And then it got cooler. I thought at first it was just the evening, but I could see now it was also the altitude – and the weather. The warmth had gone out of the air and the sky was darkening. The three of us drew closer. I untied the rugby shirt from round my waist and wriggled into it. We trudged on.

The fog seemed to come on us all of a sudden. Perversely, I was glad. Up till now, the Challenge hadn't felt like much of a challenge. Now we were having to get out our waterproofs and Robert was checking his compass. There were rocks to pick our way through and at last I felt as if I was on a mountain. I stopped thinking about the Challenge and had to concentrate on each step, watching where I placed my feet. Twisting an ankle at this stage would be a tragedy.

Then Calvin said, 'I need to have a pee.'

I joked, 'I told you not to drink all that Fanta before.'

Robert instructed him not to go too far, and we hung around, waiting for him. The fog was so thick now we had to stay close together just to be visible. As we had hoods on, even sounds were muffled. I shivered. It was like we'd moved from summer to winter in the space of a couple of hours. We waited.

After a while, I said to Robert, 'Do you think he's all right?'

'He'll have lost his way,' Robert muttered.

I shouted Calvin's name, but my voice didn't seem to carry. Robert told me to wait exactly where I was and he'd go and have a look. So there I was, standing alone in the fog, nearly at the top of Ben Nevis, and for a few moments I experienced the shock of total isolation, as if I'd become detached from the real, everyday world and was somewhere else. It was eerie; I felt vulnerable. I waited, getting more nervous by the minute. I wasn't *really* worried, but the situation spooked me.

Surely Calvin hadn't come to any harm?

I got out my torch, flashed it around. Relief surged

through me as I caught the image of Robert and Calvin together. The kid had just had a bit of bother finding us again.

'Not to worry,' Robert said. 'That was only fifteen minutes. We're still on schedule.'

Now the going was tough. There were false summits and the path was steep. We were clambering through rocks and had to go slowly, more slowly than we'd planned. Robert had to lead the way and the visibility was appalling. As the mist eddied, I noticed flecks of snow. Now I could understand why men had lost their lives up here. I thought about the contrast between the sunny afternoon we'd left just a couple of hours ago and this hostile world of rocks and fog. Funny how they were so close together.

As I shivered and felt my heart pounding, it came over me how wrong people were about nature. It wasn't all about flowers and birds and leafy trees – Ben Nevis felt like it didn't *want* to be climbed. It was pissed off that we were making our way to the top. We were fighting it. *I* was fighting it. And that felt good.

It was weird, but reaching the summit was a bit of an anticlimax. Robert announced that we'd done it, Calvin got out his camera – which was silly as we could hardly see anything – and I rested by the trig point, checking how I felt. I felt okay. My training had paid off. I got a Mars bar out of my rucksack and made short work of it, washing it down with some water, and then insisted we all began the descent.

We didn't have much time to mess about. I was glad – I just wanted to be somewhere warm.

We couldn't go that quickly. We had to pick our way carefully. Calvin pointed out gullies of snow, which Robert said were there from last winter. It struck me that last winter was when Simon had his accident. Then, the snow had been falling here; back on the school rugby pitch, he'd leapt up for the ball and that was that. But it was stupid to think that way. It was history. We were moving on.

I was impatient. I thought the descent would be much quicker, but because of the risk of falling and the tension in our legs as we braced them for each downward step, we seemed to be taking ages. It was then that Calvin decided to tell us about the time when he was bullied; I don't know why he chose then – perhaps climbing Ben Nevis had made him able to talk about it properly for the first time.

It was pretty pathetic. A boy called Tony Melton was the ringleader. It started with name-calling, then there was a scuffle outside school. When they got changed for Games, they'd poke fun at him for being fat. Then one day they invited Calvin to have a smoke on the way back from school; but once they'd lit a cigarette, this Tony grabbed it and shoved it against Calvin's wrist. At that point Calvin told his dad. His dad went into school, Tony was excluded, and then allowed back in on a 'one strike and you're out' basis. Calvin was saying he still didn't trust him and wished he'd been expelled. Robert said nothing.

But his tale made the time pass, and soon the path evened out, the fog dispersed as suddenly as it arrived, and the knowledge that we'd almost done our first peak lifted our spirits. All three of us shared a sense of elation, despite our aching calves.

'One down, two to go,' Robert said.

'We're a third of the way through,' Calvin added.

'If we can keep this pace up, we're sorted,' I said.

Inane, I know, but the exhilaration we were feeling just spilled over into pointless chatter. Other walkers caught up with us as we made our way back to the car and we all compared notes. I was feeling good. We raced down the path on the lower slopes, eager to be back at base.

John and Sylvia greeted us at the bottom with hot soup they'd prepared on the primus stove. Soup had never tasted so good. But before I could wolf down the sandwiches, John insisted we should get on our way. Night was falling, the roads would be relatively empty, and time saved travelling was time we could use on the mountains.

So we were off, heading south. I texted Wilko with our progress and hoped he'd pass the news on. It was quarter to eleven, and I guessed he'd be in the pub. I regretted not having a can of something now, but Robert had vetoed alcohol. He said it led to dehydration and that would be a disaster. So I had to grab some sleep without any artificial aids. I stretched myself out at the back of the car, and put a blanket over my body. But sleep wouldn't come.

Calvin wittered on endlessly, explaining to anyone who would listen exactly what happened when he got lost on Ben Nevis, then Robert insisted on playing a tape of sad old Eighties music he'd brought. Even when it was midnight and it had quietened down, I was too keyed up to sleep. Images of the mountain we'd climbed drifted into my mind and I thought about what lay ahead. The consciousness of what we had to do tomorrow kept my mind uncomfortably alert.

It was dark outside and the Galaxy rode smoothly through the night. I closed my eyes, forcing myself to have some kind of rest. I wondered what Emma was doing. She'd said she was going out with the girls – had she? Or did she cancel on them? Go home early? Was she thinking about me now? If two people thought about each other at the same time, would their thoughts meet in mid-air? Stupid, I know, but it was late at night and I was half-asleep. Then a new idea jolted me awake. Maybe part of the reason that she hadn't told Simon about me was that she hadn't truly finished with him? Maybe she would get back with him – I was only a distraction? No – that was doing her a disservice. Emma wasn't that kind of girl.

I calmed myself down by trying once more to imagine her, and then that led to imagining *being with* her – you don't want to know the rest. It's private. I wondered whether Simon fantasised about her too, all the time he was in the unit. Both of us wanting the same girl, neither of us able to have her.

Maybe I did snatch some sleep – I don't know. I remember coming out of a doze and hearing voices. Sylvia and John were talking and their words were just about audible.

'But what would people think,' Sylvia said, 'if he left home? That I didn't want to look after him?'

'It's not a case of what people think,' John said.

'I know, I know it isn't. But I'd worry all the time, knowing he was on his own.'

'You don't have to worry,' John said.

'Perhaps I never worried enough,' she said, bitterly.

'Not again, please, Sylvia. Not now.'

Despite what Emma had told me, I felt sorry for Simon's dad – for the first time. He'd made a mistake in the past, sure, but who's perfect?

'I'm sorry,' she said, but her tone suggested otherwise. 'I just want . . . I just want to make sure he's going to be all right now. How would I cope if anything else bad happened to him? John, I still feel the shock of his injury like it was yesterday. My Simon, my golden boy, all his hopes snuffed out. Every waking moment I think about the state he's in. It never leaves me. It's like I have to be his mother all over again, do all the things I used to do for him – and if I don't, I've failed. But you can't understand. It's different for fathers.'

'Do you think so?'

'Yes.'

'You're wrong, Sylvie. I've found it hard too. Too hard to cope with, sometimes. Maybe I *have* let you bear the brunt of it. But I also thought it would help you, being in the unit all the time. I thought you wouldn't want me around.' A pause. 'I've made a mess of this, haven't I, just like before. I'm sorry. But I'll make it up to both of you. I promise.'

'John . . .' she said uncertainly, and I could hear something desperate in her voice, a kind of reaching out. And I knew I had to stop listening because this was seriously private. I put the blanket over my head, drowning out their conversation, Robert's deep, regular breathing, and the little snuffles from Calvin. Eventually the Galaxy slowed down and I reckoned we were coming off the motorway and heading into the Lake District.

We arrived at the Wasdale Head camp-site as dawn was breaking. The semi-darkness had a transparent quality and I felt light-headed, as if I'd had the drink I craved last night. I guessed it was the effect of too little sleep. We got out of the Galaxy and I watched John and Sylvia – it was hard to gauge what she was thinking about what he'd said. I found myself rooting for him. But now I had to face another mountain.

Meanwhile, Robert recognised some people who'd been with us at Ben Nevis – they were raising funds for a cancer charity. He waved and wished them good luck. I watched Robert putting on his rucksack and as he straightened, I saw him wince.

'You okay?' I asked.

'A bit stiff. I put my back out the other day, playing with the kids. Don't worry, it won't be a problem.'

Calvin was yawning and, after as much coffee as we could manage, we set off.

SIMON

Dawn light illuminates my ward, and already there are the sounds of nurses going about their business. I lie there and try to work out where Dan must be. Judging by the time, he should be starting the ascent of Scafell Pike.

I've never climbed Scafell. Now I never will. But I don't let the thought bother me. I could lie here and list all the things I'll never do, and what would that achieve? Sod all. But we did have a family holiday in the Lake District once and we all went climbing. I think I must have been about David's age, or a little older. All I remember is almost getting to the top of the mountain and there was a sudden downpour, a torrential downpour. We were all soaked and laughing, as there was nothing else we could do. I stood there with my arms outstretched, trying to get as wet as possible. It was like standing in a shower. Rivulets of water ran into my eyes.

One thing I've learned, all the time I spend lying here, waiting, is how to use my imagination. I can recall certain things that have happened to me in minute detail, how things looked, smelt, sounded – maybe because I go over them so much. So it's easy for me now to tune into Dan, to try to imagine what he's going through.

He'll be ahead of the others and Calvin will be panting, trying to keep up with him. Mr Neale will be watching from the rear. The morning air will be damp but fresh and their boots will be ringing out against the track. Scafell's not a good mountain – the path is rough and rocky. They'll have to watch where they're going. There'll be false summits, too, and times when they won't be sure what path to take. What if there's a problem? What if they don't do it?

This is the first time I think of the possibility of Dan not completing the Challenge. Maybe they wouldn't be able to collect all the sponsor money. My mind slides off that and instead I imagine how Dan would feel if he failed.

In a flash I realise he mustn't fail. Before this – before my accident – Dan just messed around, trying hard at nothing. He called himself lazy, but that wasn't the truth. I reckon he was scared of failing, scared of not measuring up to some impossible standard he'd set himself. Now he's facing up to his deepest fear. He's put everything on the line and he's doing it for me. Yeah, he's doing it for me, but also for himself. And I want Dan to come through for his sake, not mine.

I have absolutely no belief at all in crap like telepathy and mind transference, but I'm sending all of *my* energy, *my* love of pushing myself beyond the limit, I'm gathering everything I've got, and sending it to Dan. I'm filling his lungs with my oxygen, swelling his muscles, helping his feet find their way along the scree-strewn path of Scafell. My mind's looking out through his eyes, seeing the steep ascent ahead; I'm speaking through his voice, urging on the others; I'm telling the sun to shine, but not too strongly; I'm pushing clouds away.

I know that Dan's heart's pounding hard, but his legs are pushing relentlessly forward and an instinct drives him up the right path. I'm thinking – *he's* thinking – victory. There's no possibility he'll fail at all. None.

I know I won't sleep now and instead I look forward with excitement to the rest of the day and our trip to Snowdon – me, Emma, Tim and his sister. We'll be there for Dan's triumph – our triumph. I use my arms to push myself up in bed and my morning starts.

DANNY

Scafell was a testing climb. Robert had insisted we take the quickest route – and it was steep. We were scrambling over loose boulders and stones in the dim morning light and I felt like we were on an assault course. There was no time to look around and take in the view, or to relate in any way to where we were. It was just our bodies versus the rocks. We had to watch every step. But my legs were like iron now and my body was moving automatically, like a machine programmed to do this. Robert was quiet but keeping up a good pace. Calvin lost his footing once or twice, apologising as he did so. Soon it was light, but a milky mist prevented us from seeing very much. For ages it felt like we were in a cocoon of fog, cut off from the rest of the world, trapped in a waking dream, struggling upwards.

'Can we have a rest?' Calvin asked.

'Okay,' I said, but frowned to myself. Time was an issue, but then, if a rest helped him regain some energy, it might be worth it. Robert had brought some Kendal mint cake for all of us and we had some. I glanced at Calvin and saw distress written on his face.

'What's up?' I asked.

'Nothing,' he said, and tried to smile. But his eyes said it all. He was finding this tough. I could see him struggling with anxiety and sheer exhaustion. He was only a kid, just David's age, and maybe he'd taken on more than he could manage. And here we were, nearly halfway through the Challenge, hitting the wall, just like marathon runners do. It was the hardest time. He needed encouragement.

'You're doing brilliantly,' I said to him. 'Isn't he, Rob?'

Mr Neale nodded. I thought a teacher's praise might bolster him.

Calvin sniffed, rubbed his eyes, then mustered a smile. 'Have you got any more of that mint cake?' he asked.

'When we get to the summit,' I told him.

He grinned now and I saw that whatever inner battle he was fighting, he'd won.

'Okay,' Calvin said.

I dug him in the ribs and he did the same to me. We heard the sounds of other climbers lower than us and that gave us the impetus to get ahead of them. And once more we were moving upwards. Then, after ages and ages, or just a moment – time was playing tricks with us – we arrived at a desolate mound of stones and rocks, and Robert said, 'We've got here.'

It was the summit. Then this really weird thing happened. As we stood there, our heart rate dropping, our breathing normalising, the mist dispersed. The clouds rolled back. Spread below us were the peaks of the Lake District.

It was an incredible sight. Bare, brown, open, undulating hills and the stillness of the lakes nestling in the valleys. The sky was a pale morning blue and the clouds were actually below us now, white wisps like smoke. It looked like the whole world was asleep – no, not asleep, but waiting for something momentous to happen. It was so awesome that even Calvin had shut up.

Then I noticed Robert had positioned himself a little way away from us. Obviously he didn't want to talk. I saw him looking out at the view. I guess he was thinking of his wife. I would, if I'd lost someone; I'd want to think about them when I was somewhere beautiful, somewhere that never changed. I'd feel closer to them.

Though it wasn't the same thing at all, I thought of Simon. I realised how much I was doing this for him – I wanted him to see this through my eyes, to share my strength. Or better still, to have this kind of experience all by himself. It wasn't an impossible dream. I'd heard of SCIs doing amazing things – piloting light aircraft, looking down on the world just as I was doing then. I exulted: there are no limits – only man-made ones, or ones that start in your head. That's what I was getting from being up on top of Scafell, so early in the morning.

'Can we get going again?' Calvin asked. 'I think I need another pee.'

I smiled to myself and eased myself off the rock.

*

When we got back to the Galaxy, John was frying sausages, bacon and eggs. I was starving. In a few moments I was tucking in, stuffing food down my throat like I'd not eaten in weeks.

Before long, we were off again and by that time I was totally disorientated. I gazed in a stupor out of the window.

After a while John asked, 'How are we doing for time?'

Robert answered: 'Not bad. Not bad at all. We're working on the assumption it'll take us another three and a half hours to get to Snowdon, and it's eight-thirty now . . .'

EMMA

Eight-thirty. I was in the kitchen, listening out for Adam's car. He said he'd drive me to the unit as his contribution to the day. It was kind of him; what spark there was – if any – between us, had long been extinguished. And looking back now, I wonder if Danny had feelings for me even then, that last day of the Christmas term – it would have explained why he'd hit out so viciously at Adam.

I checked the back door was locked and wondered where Danny was now – coming down Scafell, or on the road to Snowdon? I hoped they were all okay. I was looking forward to seeing him. I knew how difficult it would be for me, being with both him and Simon, but the happiness I'd get in being with Danny at the end of his Challenge outweighed anything else. Like the knowledge we could never, ever have the relationship we wanted.

A car engine . . . a ring at the door . . . Adam was on time. I finished locking up and in a few moments I was sitting in the front seat of his car and we were on our way.

'The traffic's not too bad,' he said, 'because sometimes even on Sunday morning—'

My phone announced a text message. I waited for Adam

to finish as it's rude to check your messages when someone else thinks they have your attention. But when he stopped to turn right, I got my phone out of my bag and pressed 'show'. There was a number – no name – and it was a number I didn't recognise. Intrigued, I opened the message.

I want 2 come home David

First I thought it was a wrong number or a joke. 'I've had a weird text,' I told Adam. David . . . David . . . I didn't have a friend called David. Then a thought struck me. Was it Simon's brother? But where did he get my number from? I remembered someone telling me he was staying with a friend for the weekend – maybe they'd fallen out. But why text *me*?

I discussed this with Adam, and he said, 'Ring him back, see what the matter is.'

So I did.

'Hello?' It was David – and he didn't sound okay.

'It's Emma – you texted me. Are you all right?'

'I don't like it here. I don't feel well.'

'Where are you? Which friend are you staying with?'

'I'm not. I'm in Blackpool.'

'Blackpool! What are you doing there?'

'We ran away.'

'What?'

'Me and Tony. It was his idea. He told his mum we were staying with Jamie Whittington, but we weren't. And we've been up all night and Tony's run off and I haven't got any money left. I want to come home.'

And then he started to cry.

'It's okay, it's okay,' I said, trying to be soothing. Then I couldn't help asking, 'Why did you ring *me*?'

'I didn't want to tell Mum,' he sniffed, 'and Dan's with them, and you were on my phone.'

And of course he wouldn't bother Simon, I thought. So it was up to me – David was going to be my responsibility. And in a way I was glad. Everyone else was on the Challenge. Now I had one too.

'Can you go to the police?' I asked him.

'No!'

'Hold on,' I said. I put my hand over the phone and explained to Adam what had happened. And I concluded: 'Adam, shall we go to Blackpool and get him?'

He thought for a while. 'Okay.'

I spoke to David again. 'Where exactly are you?'

'By the central pier.'

'I'll be there in a couple of hours.'

I carried on reassuring him, telling him to stay in safe places. Then the signal began to break up. Adam pulled over to the side of the road to check his atlas for the route. I could tell he was quite enjoying the idea of the chase. I just wanted to get to David as soon as possible – the idea of a twelve-year-old alone in Blackpool worried me. I tried to be patient while Adam worked out the best way to get there.

It didn't take him too long. In a few moments we sped off, with screeching tyres.

'Slow down!' I screamed.

He did, and as we drove along we tried to make sense of this. It was so out of character for David to do something like that. Adam asked who this Tony was, and then he added, was it Tony Melton? I said I thought it was. If so, he said, that boy spelt trouble. He'd often seen him outside the Head's office – he'd been excluded once or twice.

Then suddenly I exclaimed, 'Simon!' Because we should have been at the unit at nine, and it was nearly that now, and we were heading towards the motorway and Blackpool.

'I'd better ring him and explain,' I said.

Then I hesitated. What good would that do? Simon would be worried sick, even blaming himself. Similarly there was no point in ringing John and Sylvia. I could get to Blackpool before them. That was when I had my idea.

'Adam, listen. What if we go straight to Blackpool, pick up David, and then head to Snowdon and meet them all? That way David's safe and no one's worried.'

I could see Adam liked the idea. Everyone enjoys being a hero.

'Okay, let's do that,' he said. 'What time did you say they were planning to finish?'

'Half four or five.'

'It'll be tight, but we'll have a good try.'

'But take care,' I said.

'Don't you worry about me, babe,' Adam said. Mr Cool – but he wasn't a bad guy. He'd willingly given up his Sunday to help me rescue David.

Adam put a CD in the player and then we hit the motorway. The weather was halfway between sunshine and showers. I was still trying to understand how and why David had ended up in Blackpool. Was it a kids' prank? As in, let's all run away to the seaside and sneak a few rides? Or something else? Now I remembered David on the bus and the look of the boys he was with. I was worried. I willed the minutes away – I wanted to get there as quickly as we could.

'Poor David,' I said.

'Yeah,' Adam agreed. 'He's a nice kid.'

I hoped nothing dreadful had happened to him. Then I thought about Simon again and realised I couldn't just cancel on him without giving a reason. So I sent him a text.

SIMON

I've been ill all night. Too sick to travel. Ring you later. Sleeping now. Go without me. Love, Em

We're sitting in the car, waiting for her, when I get that text. I read it to Tim and his sister Alex, who's sitting behind the wheel.

'That's a pity,' Tim says. 'But we'd better do as the lady instructs. Get a move on, Alex.'

'Aye, aye, Cap'n.'

I frown to myself. I'm disappointed – I was looking forward to Emma's company. I wanted to show her that I was fine about our break-up; I wanted this day to demonstrate what good mates we could be. Then I'm sorry for her – sounds like she's spent the night throwing up. But – hold on – as we pull away from the hospital, I think, that's the first time Emma's ever had a stomach bug in all the time I've known her.

It occurs to me she's lying.

I push the thought away and chat to Tim and Alex. Tim's known some blokes who've done the Three Peaks and he's saying the worst bit is the end section, when it's just an ordeal. Even the fittest people begin to feel the strain then. He also says he knows of a tetra who'd had a specially adapted wheelchair made so he could climb to the top of Snowdon. Alex says that sounds cool. Alex is between her first and second year at uni – I've met her once or twice before.

Then I find I'm not listening, and thinking: maybe Emma couldn't face me, after breaking up with me. Maybe I didn't reassure her enough that I was okay with it. Because I'm certain this text was a cover-up. She says she's sleeping – that means she doesn't want me to call her back.

Or maybe she has met someone else, didn't have the guts to tell me, and is spending the day with him. No way – I could never imagine Emma doing that.

The motorway is busy. Tim says it's full of Sunday drivers – the worst sort. Half of them shouldn't be on a motorway – and then there are the caravans. But Alex is a good driver. I would be enjoying the drive, but my mind keeps straying to Emma. I know something is up. Maybe she doesn't want to be there at the end of Dan's walk. She wasn't the one who suggested coming along on this expedition to meet him. I suggested it and she'd fallen in. Maybe she doesn't actually *like* Dan much – I'd always assumed that because I liked them both, they liked each other. But that needn't be the case.

Alex slows down and we stop at a service station. A bit of a faff, both me and Tim getting out of the car. I notice, though, how skilful Tim is at hoisting himself onto his chair and that encourages me. I'll be as good as that one day. We both wheel ourselves into the service station, Alex between us. She reminds me of the nurses at the unit – totally unbothered with wheelchair-users. We have coffee and I see people giving us glances – one bloke in a wheelchair is bad enough, but two! I smile back at them.

We're back on the road, radio on. I go back to thinking about Emma, wondering if I should ring her after lunch. If she is telling the truth, then she still might be in bed. Then I wonder again why she wouldn't want to be there to greet Dan. Could it be true that she didn't like him?

I try to remember the history of their relationship. I recall Dan's seventeenth, when Emma kissed him. He looked embarrassed. I think of them both visiting me at my worst, when I was in halo traction, and they were both relating to me, not to each other. But they always seem comfortable with each other. I remember hearing about the time Danny socked Adam for kissing Emma under the mistletoe – defending *my* rights. I smile. No – Danny and Emma spend a lot of time together, because of me. There was no way they didn't get on.

Or perhaps they get on too well.

I try that one on for size. Danny and Emma coming and going in and out of the unit, joking at my bedside, taking me into town on my first visit home. I told them they were like my mum and dad – a couple. Was I picking up on something there? And that night, when I shouted at Em in the pub and she ran out – who went after her? Dan. Later that night he texted me to say she was fine and not to worry. The next morning I'd apologised to Emma, but I hadn't stopped to think about the significance of it being Dan who ran after her. On my behalf – or his?

'I can't stand that song!' Tim shouts over the music. 'Switch channels, Alex.'

She pushes a button or two. Now I imagine a scenario in which Emma can't bear to be with Dan and me when he finishes his walk because she'll give herself away. It's Dan she wants, not me. She finished with me as she's honest – Emma has always been honest. But she couldn't bring herself to tell me that she and Dan are an item – no, they couldn't be. They would never do that behind my back. If they did . . . my skin pricks at the mere thought of the size of the betrayal that would be.

But hey, I say to myself, *nothing's happened! You're an idiot, Simon Denham. Emma has a stomach bug. And here you are imagining her and Dan together. It's not just your legs that aren't working, but your mind.*

So I switch off and chat to Tim. We talk cars. He reckons with the money Dan's raising I can get something halfway decent. I've also told Tim that I want to give some of the proceeds to the unit – I don't want it all for myself. That is, when I can persuade my mum to drop the idea of the extension. I see a blue sign indicating the M56, that will take us to Chester and the Welsh borders. It's feeling real now and I'm looking forward to getting to Snowdon.

But what if – here I go again – what if they'd started to like each other, but they didn't do anything about it *because* of me?

Sometimes you get an idea and it sticks around in your head like an uninvited guest and it won't go away. So even as I start chatting to Alex about uni, plying her with questions, the consciousness that Dan and Emma might be involved with each other, or are fighting involvement, stays with me. I feel sick at the thought. How could they? And neither of them breathed a word to me. The bastards. I clench my fists hard.

Then I remind myself what Danny is doing for me, and that has the power to change the current of my mind. All that effort, planning, training, seeking sponsors – all for me. And here I am thinking that he was going to do all that and then take my girl. I am mad. Certifiably insane. Emma just has a stomach bug and Dan is speeding on his way to Snowdon.

DANNY

The traffic was at a total standstill. We were going absolutely nowhere. I just could not believe this, could not believe it. All five of us were stressed to our limit.

'It has to be an accident,' John muttered.

'Or roadworks?' suggested Sylvia. 'Maybe if we have to reduce to one lane . . .'

'There haven't been any roadwork signs,' Calvin added.

I couldn't see the point of deciding what the cause was. The fact was we were stuck on the A55, losing time rapidly. I was nearly at breaking point – I just wished I could smash something or someone. I didn't mind making the effort on the mountain: the fog, the boulders, the way my legs ached – no problem – but this enforced inactivity, not being able to get on with it, not being able to do what you have to do – that was what I couldn't handle. I started swearing to relieve the tension, a bit more loudly than I meant to.

'Steady on,' Robert said, overhearing me. Then I remembered he was really Mr Neale and that was weird.

My eyes strained over the traffic. No sign of movement. I thought of getting out and screaming, 'We're doing the

Three Peaks! Let us through!' But how stupid would that be?

After what seemed like ages the car in front of us edged forward. We did the same. Then came to a halt.

Robert spoke next. 'We've only lost thirty minutes; I know it feels like more, but it's not too bad. After Conway the roads are good – we can get all the way to Caernarfon and then it's only a short haul to Snowdon. I still think it's worth us driving that bit further and taking the Pyg trail up the mountain. It's shorter than the path from Llanberis, if a bit steeper.'

'We'll do that,' I said.

'I think that's the best thing,' Robert mused. 'So, John and Sylvia, you drop us off at Pen-y-Pass and meet us at Llanberis. We'll be coming back that way. As it's flatter, we can make better time.'

I wasn't really listening. I was silently urging the traffic forward.

Then Calvin shouted, 'There's an ambulance – it must be an accident.'

'Well, at least we know what it is,' Robert said. 'And that it'll be cleared soon. Let's hope no one's hurt. Okay, so assuming we're in this for another half an hour, we'll be an hour or so behind schedule, but even if we start our ascent at one o'clock we can still complete within twenty-four hours. But it will be tight. We started Ben Nevis at four-thirty, didn't we?'

'Four thirty-one and fourteen seconds,' Calvin amended.

'We can still do it,' Robert said.

The traffic edged forward again. I tried to steady myself by imagining telling Emma all about it, once I'd got home. I loved the way when Emma listened to you, it was with all of her attention, every bit of it. I looked forward to giving her my account of the weekend and I wondered when I would see her again. I stopped myself. Thinking of Emma hurt, hurt badly, and I was aching enough as it was. Instead I tried to focus on the moment we'd greet our reception committee – Juliet and the kids, my parents and sister, and Calvin's parents.

If, that is, we reached our target. And if this traffic didn't clear, there was a real risk we wouldn't do it. The thought of failure sickened me. It was just not an option. I'd sprint up Snowdon if need be.

Come on, you bastards, I said to the traffic. *Move, why don't you?!*

EMMA

We followed the signs to the seafront. The roads were full of cars heading in the same direction; I felt a mounting frustration and found myself leaning forward, willing the car to move more quickly. Then I thought I'd better give David another ring and assure him we were nearly there. That would give me something to do.

I rang his number and got the voicemail message. So I tried again. And again. He'd switched off his phone, which was crazy, as he knew we were on our way. Why had he done that? What if . . . what if someone had stolen his phone or . . . he'd run out of battery, or maybe something had happened to him? I could feel myself panicking. I gripped onto the side of the car.

'He's switched off,' I told Adam, but he was too busy negotiating the roads.

So we crawled along, passing hordes of holidaymakers. Normally I love being at the seaside; I love all the tat on sale in shops, the sticks of rock, the silly hats, the tacky souvenirs, the smell of fish and chips and salty sea air – it makes me feel like a kid again. But now it was just a noisy, heaving, dangerous sort of place. The weather wasn't that good either – it was overcast, threatening rain.

After what seemed like ages, we got out onto the front. The cars formed one slow line of traffic, inching along. There was absolutely nowhere we could park. I knew we should have thought about that before, but normally that's the kind of thing parents think about, not us. So Adam said he'd drop me off at the central pier, I'd collect David, he'd circle round and pick us up. That sounded sensible.

Eventually we got there. I leapt out of the car and looked around me. There were quite a few people and my eyes tried to pick out the familiar figure of David. He wasn't there. I saw a woman with a gaggle of kids, an old couple arm-in-arm, and behind them the garish entrance to the pier with its stalls and a café nearby – but no David. I looked again, all around me, over the road, both ways along the seafront. Nothing. No one. I thought he might be in the café, so I entered. It was crowded with families eating, but there was no sign of David. Panicking properly now, I asked a few people if they'd seen a boy around twelve, short fair hair, and, no, I didn't know what he was wearing, but I guessed he must have looked upset. There were just blank faces in response.

Outside it was beginning to drizzle. I surveyed the various people seeking shelter from the rain, but it was no use. David wasn't here. So I got my phone and rang him. Still only the voicemail message in response. I stood by the side of the road redialling frantically, looking out for Adam's car. Eventually it came into view. I leapt in and explained the situation.

'I think we ought to go to the police,' Adam said.

I had to admit that seemed the only thing we could do. But where was the police station? I'd been to Blackpool only two or three times in my life and didn't have a clue where it was situated. We decided to head back to the town centre and ask someone. But even that was a problem. The holiday traffic was so bad we hardly moved. Meanwhile I wondered what could have happened to David. I was torn between anger that he hadn't stayed by the pier and fear that something had gone badly wrong. What if someone had offered to help him, but had had other plans? What if Tony had come back and taken him somewhere else?

I scanned everyone as we drove along. Then I saw him – he was looking in the window of a souvenir shop. He had his back to us – he was wearing a stripy T-shirt. I told Adam to stop and he pulled into the kerb, putting on his hazard lights. I jumped out of the car and grabbed the boy. But it wasn't David. I blushed and apologised; he just looked at me as if I was weird.

'Please,' I said aloud. 'Can somebody help?'

A woman in lime green shorts and a pink sun-top approached me and I asked her where the police station was. She didn't know either. I could hear the clink of machines from the amusement arcade nearby. Adam hooted on the horn of his car.

I could see this was going to be impossible. Maybe I ought

to ring John and Sylvia – this was becoming more serious by the minute.

'Emma!'

I swivelled round. Coming towards me was David, in a blue baseball cap. He looked pale and dishevelled. I screamed his name and hugged him. He hugged me back and buried his face in my chest. Adam hooted some more.

'Get in the car!' I ordered David. I bundled him into the back seat, and got in the back with him.

'Don't you have anything with you, any overnight things?' I asked, puzzled.

He shook his head. I could see his eyes were glistening with tears. I hate it when boys cry. It rips me up inside – and little boys are worst of all. I hushed him and hugged him while Adam pulled out into the line of traffic. I trusted him to get us out of Blackpool and on the road to Wales.

Once David had calmed down and my pulse had stopped racing, I asked David to tell me exactly what had happened.

'It was Tony's idea. He said it would be fun to have a weekend in Blackpool. He had enough money for a ticket on the trains. He said we could sleep on the beach and no one would see us. I thought it would be an adventure – and nobody cared where I was, anyway.'

'Of course people care.'

He ignored that.

'So when we got here it was ace. We went on the Pleasure Beach and spent our money on rides and drinks. Then we walked into town and Tony got these lads to buy us some cider.'

'But you're only twelve!'

'And we drank that and I was sick. I said to Tony, can we get the train home? But he said he'd lost our tickets. I got upset and he was screaming at me, calling me names. Then he ran off. I don't know where he went. It was late then and I didn't know where to go. I walked around until I got tired and I found a doorway at the back of a café and I sat there for a bit, but I was frightened to sleep in case somebody got me.'

'Oh my God!'

Then in the morning I went down to the beach – and that bit was okay, seeing the waves come in, pretending I was on holiday. I was hungry but I didn't have any money left. Emma, I did something wrong – I took some money from my mum's purse.'

'You did a lot of things wrong,' I told him.

'Then I rang you, and you said you'd come for me. Then Tony started texting me, horrible things, saying he'd beat me up for wimping out. That's why I turned my phone off. And there was a man by the pier who kept staring at me, so that's why I went for a walk.'

'It's lucky I found you!'

'Don't tell Mum and Dad, please.'

I was silent. I couldn't make that promise to him. It didn't seem right that his parents shouldn't know. He read my silence correctly.

'They'll kill me!'

'No, they won't. But they *will* be upset and you'll have to talk to them and tell them why you did it.'

'I thought about running away before. It was horrible after Simon's accident. Mum was always at the hospital and Dad locked himself in his study. They got me DVDs to watch but . . . Emma, I'm really hungry.'

'Can we stop for some food?' I asked Adam.

'Sure,' he said. 'But we'd better be quick. We've got to get back onto the motorway, then take the M6 to Chester, and we've still got miles to go.'

We pulled in at a garage and, while Adam filled up, I bought sandwiches, crisps and drinks for us all. We parked the car in the corner and ate, knowing we wouldn't have another chance. David was still eating as we drove away.

Before too long he'd finished and within ten, maybe even five minutes, he was fast asleep, his head lolling on one side, his mouth open. After a while he jerked, adjusted his position, and leant against me. I was frightened to move in case I disturbed him.

Adam spoke to me from the front. 'He's crazy.'

'No,' I whispered, not wanting to wake David up. 'Not crazy. I feel a bit sorry for him.' My voice trailed away. To be honest, I felt confused. David had been stupid, running away like that, stupid and selfish. He knew how much the Challenge meant to everyone, and to choose *this* weekend to do something so daft! Then an uncomfortable thought kept nudging at me – *had* David been neglected? Had Sylvia and John's concern for Simon taken David out of their line of vision? Did they think their younger son would be able to look after himself? Because if they did, they were wrong. The enormity of the whole situation broke upon me and, though I was glad we had David safe and sound, I could see this was only the beginning.

David whimpered in his sleep. I brushed his hair from his forehead. It fell like Simon's did and I could almost imagine it was Simon I was stroking, a young Simon, before his accident. That accident, I realised, had sent out ripples that had affected us all, changed all of our lives. We'd all grown older because of it – well, me, Simon and Dan had. I could even see now how the love I'd felt for Simon was a kid's love. In the beginning I was thrilled he fancied me, because I fancied him; we were the same age, the same type, everyone approved of us. It all felt so right and easy.

Now it was no longer easy, or right. And what I felt for Dan was the opposite – wrong and difficult. And because of that, it was so much more intense and irresistible. No – there was more to it. I'd grown to know Danny better than I'd ever truly known Simon. I'd seen him upset, angry, in a foul temper, sweaty after a run, falling asleep in front of the video at my house – and I still loved him.

But I would just have to love him in secret.

DANNY

We walked out of the Pen-y-Pass car park at one-thirty. Our original plan had been to leave four and a half hours for Snowdon – because of the bad traffic we now had just three. But Robert was optimistic and I was determined. Calvin was as chatty as ever.

'It's good that we could leave our rucksacks in the car. It's easier walking when you're lighter. Will we see that lake, Sir, the one that's coloured blue from all the copper? That's on the other side of the mountain, so we might see it coming down. I read that—'

'Shut up, Calvin, and move, move, move!' I barked.

I ran ahead, urging him on. I reckoned it might be a good idea to jog the distance until the climb began in earnest and Robert agreed. I glanced up at the sky. It was difficult to predict what the weather was going to do. There were patches of blue sky, but also a shroud of white mist and one, large, more ominous grey cloud. So what if it rained? We would get wet – big deal.

My legs were aching and I could feel the effort the climb was taking. I thought by this stage I'd be euphoric, thinking how near we were to our goal, but instead I just wanted to get the whole bloody thing over and done with. I can't say I noticed the view; I was just intent on pushing myself, encouraging the others and making as good time as it was humanly possible. I used other walkers on the path as pacemakers – I'd see a couple of hikers and think: we'll overtake them – and that spurred me on. And there were certainly a lot of walkers, more than on the other mountains. But then, it was a Sunday afternoon, reasonable weather and Snowdon is a popular tourist resort – it even had a railway going to the top. I saw a plume of smoke from the train in the distance, and I resented all the lazy sods who were sitting in it and not walking to the top. Like us.

It seemed like a long haul. I reckon I could have sprinted up, but I was aware that Robert and Calvin were finding it tougher than me. As we ascended, the sun faded. The clouds rolled over; a light rain fell. Then the mist came. Even if I'd had time to appreciate the view, I couldn't have.

Eventually we zig-zagged up the ridge leading to the summit and turned left, Robert assuring us we didn't have far to go. Which was good to hear – because I couldn't tell where on earth we were. The mist was so thick that I could only see the walkers in front of us. That slowed us down, as did the fact that the summit of Snowdon, with its little café, was heaving with people. It just seemed so surreal – to have a café smelling of baked beans and tea sitting on the top of the highest mountain in Wales. Then, out of the mist, I heard the clacking of the train and saw the mist thicken as it was joined by the smoke from the engine.

We picked our way to the top and now Robert pushed on, making for the trig point on the summit. He knew Snowdon – he'd climbed it once or twice before. In the murky mist we followed him up a slate-ridden slope to a small mound, with steps carved into it, leading to a platform where people were huddled round a fat stone pillar with a diagram of the view etched on it. What view? It was all mist.

So we were there – on the summit. The hardest part was over; it was all nearly over.

'We've got one hour twenty minutes for the descent,' Robert warned. 'It's going to be tight. Let's go for it.'

So we turned to head back to Llanberis. One hour twenty. What if we didn't make it in time? There'd be no way of hiding it. At the bottom of Snowdon were my mum and dad, Calvin's dad with his camcorder, Juliet taking pictures for the school magazine, and Simon's mum and dad – his representatives. They were all following our progress, minute by minute. If we were late, they would know. More to the point, if we were late, Simon would know. He always plays fair. What would he say if we all lied to get his money? The whole thing would stink.

No, we couldn't cheat even if we wanted to. We were doing this for the money, yeah, but I was starting to see there was more to it than that. We were also doing the Three Peaks for us. Us alone. We needed to know we finished it in under twenty-four hours so we could look our sponsors in the eye and demand the cash. Personal pride was at stake here. My pride. I had to do this in the time we said, or it wouldn't be worth doing.

There wasn't a second to spare.

SIMON

We wheel ourselves out of the car park and cross the road to the mountain railway station. It's pretty tacky: tables and chairs with umbrellas over them, a café, a takeaway, and the obligatory gift shop. There's a train at the platform now. I can't see it but I do notice the column of greeny-yellow smoke it belches from its funnel. There are hordes of people but magically they all make way for us. Alex makes some enquiries and finds out where the path down Snowdon ends. I tell her I'd like to go and wait there, to see Dan and the others as they come down. We all agree it's a good idea. I guess my parents are around somewhere, but we'll meet up soon enough.

So we follow Alex up along the main road and round the corner down a terrace of houses to a triangle of lawn with a bench. She sits there and Tim and I park our chairs by her. It's half past three. I know Dan must be down by half four, as Wilko texted me to keep me informed of their progress. We haven't missed them as Mum called earlier saying they were a little behind schedule.

I see ahead of me a cattle grid with a gate by the side for pedestrians, and watch a steady stream of people enter and exit. There are all sorts: dedicated walkers with walking poles and rucksacks with water bottles peeping out of pockets on each side; parties of Japanese tourists; and even tattooed blokes in T-shirts who look like they've taken the wrong turn to the pub. My eyes are trained on the upward path beyond the cattle grid for any sign of Dan. Just for one moment, I wish I was with him and it hits me, full-on, that I'll never be able to climb a mountain by myself. I experience that yearning, feel the pain, then let it go. Alex asks if we want anything, a drink? Something to eat? I shake my head.

I wonder what Dan's doing up there? Is he struggling? Are the others okay? I still can't believe that all of this is in aid of me and I realise that, whatever happens in the future, I'll never be alone – not with friends like Dan. And Emma. And the uncomfortable thought I've been having intermittently all day comes back to me: Dan and Emma. Dan and Emma.

I hear my mother's voice calling me, turn my chair round, and there she is with Dad, ready to meet the descending party. As soon as I see her I detect a change in her face. She looks happy – happier than I've seen her for ages. I know something has happened but I can't think what. She bends down, kisses me; Dad shakes hands with Tim, is introduced to Alex. We discuss Dan's progress and agree they're leaving it late. I feel myself tensing. I want them to do it. My mind switches into rugby mode, where all my focus is on making the thing happen that I want to happen. So at first I hardly catch my mother's words.

'Simon, it's okay. We're not building that extension.'

I switch back to the real word. Say, lamely, 'What?'

'You ought to go away to university. I can see that.'

I'm confused. I frown. She says, 'Dad thinks – and so do I – that you ought to try to manage by yourself.'

I glance at Dad. I know immediately something has passed between them. I sense a connection renewed – they look like my mum and dad used to look before that business three years ago. They're a couple again. I don't ask what has happened – in fact, I discover I don't even want to know. I realise I feel safe in my family again – even as they're giving me my freedom – and I wish David was here to see this.

My dad says, 'They've only got forty minutes.'

It's true. For the first time I think something could have seriously delayed them. I wonder what. Snowdon is the least formidable of the three peaks. If you're sensible up there, little can go wrong. My eyes scan the descending walkers, more and more of them now as the afternoon wears on. But no sign of Dan. None at all.

EMMA

We didn't know where to go when we got to Llanberis. The village was strung out along the main road and Adam kept going into the wrong car parks. I saw a vast mountain looming over me to the left. It had been savagely cut into, with layers of slate exposed, like a kind of quarry. Snowdon was so close I couldn't see its summit. David had woken about ten minutes ago and was still bleary-eyed. Adam wound down his window to ask a man where to go to find the Snowdon path.

The man answered in a faint sing-song Welsh accent. He directed us to a car park a little further along. I checked my watch. Ten to four. We might even be too late to meet them. At the idea of not being there to see Danny finish, my heart gave a sudden lurch.

Before too long we were parked and the three of us made our way across the road past the railway station, following the directions the man had given us. I was reassuring David that I'd make sure his mum and dad weren't too angry, as we turned into a street with houses on one side with black-and-white gables. Adam commented that the number of walkers coming along it meant it must be the right place.

I saw immediately we were in time to meet them, as there was John and Sylvia, and also Simon, Tiny Tim and a girl. They were talking to a woman with two kids. David took my hand and held it tight. We approached them. There was real astonishment at our appearance, exclamations all round.

Simon said to me, 'I thought you were ill.'

'No, we had to rescue David.'

'*Rescue?*'

'I'll explain later.'

For now I decided the best thing to do was make light of it. I told Sylvia that David wasn't having a very nice time with his friend – they'd fallen out and he rang me, knowing his parents weren't able to fetch him. I didn't want to spoil the end of the Challenge. But I knew that later on everyone would have to face the truth. It was just that now wasn't that time.

Before too long Danny's parents and his sister Katy arrived, along with another couple who I guessed were Calvin's parents. We were such a crowd that people were turning to look at us. I stood by Simon.

'They've got twenty minutes,' he said.

'That's not long.'

'I'd have thought they would have been back before now.'

I agreed with him, then said, 'Do you think they're all right?'

'I hope so.'

Now this is crazy – I'm not normally a worrier – but ever since Simon's accident I immediately imagine the worst that can happen, almost to reassure myself that it won't. Mountains are dangerous. What if one of them had fallen; slipped down a sheer slope? What if Dan was hurt?

'Dan will be okay, won't he?' I asked, unable to stop myself.

Simon said nothing, but gave me a sidelong glance.

SIMON

That was when I knew for sure. Maybe it was the way she said his name. Or perhaps just that he was the one she picked out. Or I just have a sixth sense about these things. Now it had come to this point, I would have to find out the truth. Although there were lots of people around, no one was paying us any attention. We were effectively on our own.

'Dan'll be okay,' I say. 'And Calvin. And Mr Neale.'

I see a muscle jump in her throat. I carry on now and I don't care if I hurt her because I have to know. She owes it to me to tell me the truth.

'But really it's Dan you're worried about, isn't it?'

Emma says nothing but her skin flushes.

'Are you seeing him?'

'No!' she says immediately, almost cutting into my question.

And, just as quickly, I say, 'But you'd like to. You'd both like to be with each other. But you won't because of me.'

As I say these words I still don't know if they're true or not. I'm like a detective at the end of a case confronting the guilty party with a scenario, testing my hypothesis.

Emma's silence tells me all I need to know. I've guessed right. First, I get some pleasure from the fact I've been smart, that I've worked it out for myself. Then a wave of rage crashes into me and I can't see straight. All I think is: how could they do this to me?

'So all the time I've been struggling to get out of the unit, you and Dan have been pretending to be there for me, but it's each other you've really been into.'

'No! You've got it all wrong! You don't understand.'

'I understand perfectly,' I say bitterly. I want to hurt Emma. I want to hurt her like she's hurt me. 'I've been cheated on by both of you.'

'Is that what you think?' Suddenly she turns on me, her eyes blazing. 'God, Simon, you *have* changed. You're seeing it in the worst possible light. Just listen. It's true, Dan and I *do* have feelings for each other. But we've done nothing about them *because* of you. Because we both love you and that comes first. It's why we're not together. It's why Dan is slogging his guts out on that mountain – for you. No one's betrayed you here. You're doing this to yourself.'

I don't take in what she's saying. I grip the sides of my chair hard. Emma and Dan. Emma and Dan. And then me, left out of the frame. I don't think I can handle this.

DANNY

We couldn't go as quickly as we would have liked on the descent because the path was so uneven; there were loose stones and rocks everywhere. Robert said that because we were tired, there was every chance we could slip. It was frustrating, not being able to run helter-skelter down the mountain. I had cramp in the front of my thighs – it felt like the muscles in my legs had turned to metal and wouldn't give. The backs of my calves were aching too. This was just hell, pure and simple.

But the mist suddenly lifted, as if it had never been there. On my left there was a panorama of mountains, peak after peak, each peeping from behind the other. A whole expanse of Welsh countryside, beautiful and forbidding. But there was still some ground to cover. When Robert moved ahead of us, I could tell he was worried about time. Both Calvin and I skirted round a group of walkers to keep up with him.

'I thought you said this path was flatter,' I accused Robert.

'It is – we'll be able to make better time lower down,' he panted.

We passed the halfway house café, with groups of walkers sitting outside, drinking bottles of water. I was thirsty too and knew I ought to drink, but there wasn't the time. I didn't look at my watch, but Calvin did.

'Thirty-three minutes,' he said. 'I'm going to run.'

The ground was levelling out now and there were fewer loose stones and uneven patches. I reckoned it might be an idea to race Calvin. I watched him skitter ahead down the path, then suddenly disappear from view. I ran forward a few paces. He was writhing on the ground.

In a moment Robert and I were bending over him.

'What happened?' Robert asked urgently.

Calvin's face was white. You could see the pain written on his face. My mind ricocheted back to Simon's accident and I had to tell myself this was different.

'It's my ankle,' he moaned.

Only his ankle. This one I could deal with.

'Can you walk?' I asked.

He struggled to his feet, attempted to stand, and half-collapsed.

'No,' he said. By this time a few interested walkers had come to gawp.

Robert took over. He manipulated Calvin's ankle. 'It feels like a sprain. He won't be able to finish,' Robert told me. 'I'll stay with him. You go on down and complete. Then get some help and we'll have him carried down. I'd do it, but my back isn't up to it.'

Part of me did want to hare off down the mountain. Then I remembered how much money was riding on Calvin. I tried to imagine how it would be for him going round to sponsors and saying, 'I didn't complete the Challenge, but do you mind giving your money anyway?' Utterly humiliating. No, Calvin – all of us – had to finish this, and finish within twenty-four hours. There was only one solution.

I ordered Robert: 'Get him onto my back.'

'You can't possibly carry him down, Dan. We're still thirty minutes from the bottom and you couldn't bear the weight – not in the state you're in.'

'Get – him – on – my – back!' You should try shouting at a teacher – it feels very, very good.

Against his better judgement, Robert hoisted Calvin onto me. The kid clung round my neck and locked his legs round my waist. He was heavier than I'd anticipated. But I didn't care, he was Simon's car, he was my lucky mascot, he was my mate Calvin and also – *he was Simon.* I wanted to be carrying him down. The aches and pains in my body vanished. My willpower took over. I strode down the mountain, people making way for me.

'Fifteen minutes,' Robert gasped, pushing to keep up with me.

'Ride 'em, cowboy!' Calvin shouted.

Then we saw a queue of people – a queue? They were waiting to get over a stile. Robert pushed to the front, explaining our situation. A big bloke lifted Calvin off me as I climbed the stile and then placed him back on. And once again we were off. I was hell-bent on doing this.

Suddenly the path revealed a view of Llanberis, nestling by the side of the lake, a higgledy-piggledy collection of white-walled, slate-roofed houses. Somewhere down there was our greeting party, anxiously checking their watches. It couldn't be far now.

'Twelve minutes,' Robert said.

I raced off, Robert jogging by my side. This was going to be tight. I only had one objective. Everything hung on speed. I ignored my body crying out in agony.

We turned into a tarmac road. 'We must be nearly there,' I gasped.

'Not quite,' Robert puffed. He was running, so I realised I must be running too. The road was steep. I was frightened of collapsing with Calvin on top of me. Then we had to slow as a car edged its way past us going up the track. The driver wound down his window.

'Want any help?'

Robert shouted, 'No!'

That was valuable time lost. We carried on our headlong rush, Calvin's feet banging against my sides, his grip on my neck uncomfortably tight. The path curved to the right and still there seemed to be no end, no sight of our greeting party.

We *must* be almost there.

SIMON

I look straight ahead of me. Everyone thinks I'm watching for Danny, but I'm struggling to accept this new – this *old* – turn of events. Emma and Dan. Am I being unreasonable? I thought I didn't mind Emma breaking up with me, but the thought that it was because of Dan makes it different. She should have said. I glance at her. She's crying. Tears rolling down her cheeks.

Her tears check my anger. What has she done wrong? Nothing. You can't help your feelings. Or can you? What had Dan done wrong? Nothing. It was all an accident. Even in this turmoil I could see they hadn't plotted against me or meant to hurt me. What a bloody mess.

I breathe out, long and hard. I check my watch. My heart sinks. It's half past four. They haven't done it.

I never imagined this. It's never crossed my mind that Danny was going to fail this challenge. In the midst of my anger I feel a rush of disappointment for him. Emma wipes her face with her hand, and automatically I reach out and take her damp hand, hold it, then squeeze it. That makes me feel better, but I hardly know why it should.

David and Katy are standing near the cattle grid where they have a better view.

'They're coming! They're coming!' David shouts.

We all look. There, running at top speed, is Dan, with Calvin clinging to his back, Mr Neale jogging by his side. David holds open the gate for them, Danny runs out, squats down, and Calvin lands on the ground, checking his watch as he does so.

'Four thirty-one precisely,' he shouts. 'We've done it!'

Calvin reaches for his ankle while Mr Neale strides forward to talk to all of us. I watch Danny, who straightens himself and re-orientates.

I drop Emma's hand. I know she wants to be with Dan. But she stays rooted to the spot. I feel guilty now. I've upset her. Then Dan sees me – I watch his whole face brighten. My throat seizes up. I don't know what to say to him. Thank you for taking my girl? You bastard, you've climbed the Three Peaks for me?

Dan comes over to me and Emma. 'Done it,' he says.

Now the challenge is mine. Can I rise to it? I don't know.

'Thanks,' I say. 'And by the way, I know about you and Emma.'

Dan's eyes lock onto mine and out of the corner of my vision I see the others coming up to congratulate him. We don't have long.

Dan's words stumble out. 'I didn't mean it to happen.'

'I know,' I say. 'It's okay.'

It isn't, not yet, but for now I'm going to pretend that it is. I can do it, because I'm tougher than I've ever been. I'm crippled on the outside, but inside I'm stronger than ever.

Dan's eyes dart from mine, to Emma's. 'You told him?'

'He knew anyway,' she says.

Dan crouches down by my chair and there are tears in his eyes.

'Are you sure?' he asks me.

'Yeah,' I say, 'but let's not talk about it now.'

He hugs me and I hug him back.

I *will* be able to handle this because I don't want to lose the two best friends I'll ever have.

EMMA

That was a year ago – that day when Danny finished the Three Peaks and Simon found out about us. It's still crystal-clear in my mind. All three of us were so staggered by everything that had happened that we were just numb as all the parents and kids came up and cheered us, and passers-by looked on and grinned. I didn't know whether to go up to Dan or not. I thought it would be better if I kept my distance. I didn't want to upset Simon and, besides, we'd have to explain to everyone else.

But once, I stole a glance at Dan – sunburnt, sweat plastering down his hair, in need of a shave, his clothes crumpled and sodden, Simon's rugby shirt still tied round his waist – and I thought he'd never seemed more handsome to me. He must have known I was looking at him, as he raised his eyes and we smiled at each other. My heart pounded so hard, it almost stopped me breathing. But we said nothing. There was no need.

That's been the tone of our relationship since – we've kept everything low key, to give Simon time to get used to it. We all talked it through endlessly. And it was painful. But there was so much to occupy Simon on his return home, so much else to think about, that bit by bit we all adjusted.

Hard to think it's been a whole year. And here I am now, standing in front of my bedroom mirror in a flowery dress that Mum says is perfect for a wedding – and I feel eighteen going on forty. But then, I quite like taking on a role, so I don't mind. Again I remember that in a month or two, I'll be starting drama school – in London. I'm scared, but it's what I want to do, I'm sure of that. And if all goes well with his A2s, Dan will be in London too.

Maybe it will be easier, if we're both together in a different city. All year we've had to downplay our relationship in front of Simon, in front of everyone.

Simon and I are still good friends – I saw a lot of him once he'd moved home and we all began to deal with what had happened to David. Although Sylvia and John were quick to reassure him they weren't angry, he wasn't okay for ages. He skipped school, saying he felt sick. So they took him to the doctors' and they ran tests, but they couldn't find anything wrong. So in the end they arranged for him to see a counsellor. Dan and Simon didn't think it was necessary but I reckon Sylvia felt guilty and, by arranging the counsellor, she felt she was doing something useful. Bit by bit David got back to normal, and things took a turn for the better when the Head 'persuaded' Tony Melton to move to another school.

There was one other difficult time – when Mr Smith

approached David and asked if he'd like to try for the rugby team. In the end it was Simon who told him he ought to do it, and when David played in his first match, Si and I were there together to watch him. The hardest part was the sympathetic glances all the spectators gave us. I thought: we don't need your sympathy. We've all learned more than you'll ever know.

Mum knocks at my bedroom door and asks if I'm ready. I invite her in and she makes a fuss, telling me how nice I look, and how she'll drive me to Dan's place. I ask her to fasten the locket that Dan bought me for my eighteenth, and she does so, and I smile as the cool silver chain settles and rests on my neck.

DANNY

Robert had insisted on a carnation. I told him I felt like a real dickhead, but he said an usher at a wedding always wore a carnation as a buttonhole. Emma fixed it, said it was sweet, and she kissed me.

I hoped Robert and Juliet's wedding wasn't going to give her any ideas. I told her that and she laughed. She was still set on a career on the stage, all the more so as she'd got her place at drama school. I was also going to London in a month, A2 results permitting. I did work pretty hard – well, I worked pretty hard towards the end. Well, okay, for the last week. Once Emma and Simon read me the riot act.

We walked to the church ahead of my family. It was a warm August afternoon, lazy sun and a light breeze. We were chatting about this and that; I told her that Pete's wife had had another baby – a little girl – who they'd called Harley. I chuckled. 'I think that's a cool name,' Emma said.

When we got to the church Simon and Calvin were already there. They were the other ushers and also – I was glad to see – wearing carnations. We all greeted each other; we were all pretty nervous doing this, but Robert had insisted we do it for him – and none of us felt we could refuse. Robert came up to say hello and he looked pretty excited. The big white wedding thing was mainly for Juliet – this was her first and only marriage, and she'd wanted the works since she was a kid.

Emma and I stood at the back of the church, enjoying being alone for just a moment. Our hands met and we interlocked our fingers. I felt a rush of happiness and my eyes sought out Simon. He grinned at me, and Emma and I didn't let go of each other's hands.

SIMON

I see them holding hands and I realise that my good mood isn't dented at all. Not for the first time, I think: I've come to terms with this – and I like myself because of it. Emma breaks away now and hurries over to me. I can see she has something to tell me, and can't wait.

'Jen's been speaking to Claire,' she says. 'She's waiting for you to ring. Do it. Do it this afternoon!'

I grin. I guess she's probably right. Claire's a girl in my Chemistry group. Dropping back a year at school meant I had to make a new set of friends, and Claire just happens to be one of them. She's been sending me signals that she's interested and at first I ignored them, but everyone's been on at me to make a move.

'I'll text her later,' I say, and decide that I definitely will. But for now I have a job to do. I'm an usher, and I have to greet the guests and indicate where they should go. I turn and move into the church.

That's when it hits me, an overpowering feeling of happiness. Maybe it's got something to do with my confidence about the AS results due out soon, or the fact

I have a driving test next week and I'm sure I'll pass. Or maybe it's what Emma said about Claire.

Yes, it's all of those, but it's also something more. Just for one moment, the everyday hassles I have just slip away and I'm glad to be me. I honestly wouldn't want to be anyone else, or any different to the way I am now. I'm not saying it's easy being a tetra – life can be pretty grim sometimes. But not all the time. And certainly not at this particular moment.

I relish the coolness of the church, the sight of the flowers, the buzz of excited chatter. I see Danny walk up the aisle with Robert Neale in tow. I glance at my parents together in one of the back pews and smile.

Everything's going to be all right.

FURTHER INFORMATION

For more information about living with spinal injury, contact:

The Spinal Injuries Association
e-mail sia@spinal.co.uk
website – www.spinal.co.uk

The SIA represents the interests of spinal cord injured people in the UK regardless of how the impairment occurred or whether it resulted in full or partial paralysis – their motto is 'because life needn't stop when you're paralysed'.

The Back-Up Trust
e-mail admin@backuptrust.org.uk
website – www.backuptrust.org.uk

Back-Up aims to support people with spinal cord injury to surpass their aspirations by offering a relationship built around peer support, mentoring and team-based outdoor activities.